CACTUS
by Anna Wilson

Published by Onlywomen Press Ltd.,
38 Mount Pleasant, London WC1.

ISBN 0 906500 04 4

Typesetting by Dark Moon

Cover: etching by Deborah Stern

Printed by Pitman Press Ltd., Bath.

Cover printed by Tenreck Ltd., London

Onlywomen Press believes it is necessary to create a women's communication system. At the very least, this would mean we could and would print our own books on our own machines with our own hands. At present, our machines are small so that if we printed this book on them the consequent binding costs would have been prohibitive. Our machines are adequate for the smaller jobs (leaflets, pamphlets, posters) which we are continuing to print for other groups. We welcome your support.

Onlywomen Press gratefully acknowledges that this book has been published with financial assistance from the Greater London Arts Association.

Anna Wilson was born in 1954 in the home counties. After a middle-class Oxford education, she was for three years a civil servant. She now lives in London with her cat and is on the editorial collective of the feminist literary magazine *Spinster*. *Cactus* is her first novel.

They walked in single file along the beach at the tide's edge, the sands long and faintly glimmering, the two women strung out apart. Eleanor felt the thread of connection cast between them, binding across the sand. She smiled at Bea's back, at its tweedy covering. There they were: two women walking on the sands after tea. Two women, their shoes sturdy, holidaying early this year, together for the first time. ('Why shouldn't we go down to the sea together, Nellie, rent a cottage, perhaps, and keep away from those boarding houses? We'd have to go in May, though, for the lower prices.') How should the world know anything of them? Eleanor glanced back along the sands — a man and a dog, small black figures in the distance. She looked back again at Bea, bending over something in the sand, and down at her hands. She smiled. That man there couldn't come near to guessing how well, how clearly her hands knew the bones of Bea's shoulder blades beneath her coat, beneath the cotton blouse so sharp to the touch. To guessing the inevitability of it, it all.

In the train going down, Bea putting her head out of the window, shrieking with laughter in the dusk, determined to have her first smell of the sea: 'We must be almost at Dawlish, surely,' she said, and put her head out. And drawing it in again a minute later, 'I had a face full of steam!' She was still laughing, and her face covered with grime from the engine.

And I, thought Eleanor, at the memory the same excitement clawing, I leaned over her in the carriage, my hand on her shoulder to steady myself, and wiped her face with my handkerchief — and that's where it started — we were laughing together so hard, I didn't want to take my hand off her shoulder, that thin delicate bone and the slope down to the neck, a hollow there, to kiss Bea there feels closer than ever to her, feels close to fragility, to the centre of her. But I didn't do that then, of course not, I hardly knew what it was I wanted, and if I did know, that couldn't mean that she'd want it too. We wouldn't have done anything without the bed at all,

1

just had a pleasant holiday, walked and read and ate — and talked perhaps — what would we have talked about? But when we got to the cottage, Bea lit the lamps and we started carrying them about — there only seemed to be three rooms, counting the kitchen, and we walked through them all more than once, and I met Bea in the front room at last and said, 'There's only one bed'.

'Yes,' she said, and bit her lip. It was her booking, through the paper. 'The notice said, "sleeps two", she said, 'and I thought —' And I saw her blush and wanted to make it better for her and I said: 'And so it will.'

Eleanor stood still on the beach, her hands in her pockets, the wind licking at her skirt, at her woollen stockings put on for the cold. All at once Beatric was beside her, not touching but close.

'I want to kiss you,' she said, grinning.

Eleanor's innards turned again. 'I want to kiss you too.'

'Well?'

'But Bea, the open!'

'Damn the open,' said Bea.

They walked back arm in arm, Eleanor clinging to Bea's arm, slowing her down slightly; she felt that she needed to arrest their progress, their whole progress, this particular walk, everything. She needed to take stock of what had happened, to finish the story in her head, to draw breath and stand back from it all for a moment. Then perhaps she would know what was to happen at the end of the week. When they went back to London. For now she could only lean on Bea's arm and slow her down, make her look at the landscape, fix it bright in her head, make each thing they did last a little longer.

'Bea, that bright bright green on the fields, look, how splendid it is! And the sun has turned the rocks pink!'

They stopped on the path to see the sun go down and the light fade from rocks and grass until only the breakers at the sea's edge shone white from the grey. Then Bea laughed across at her and shook her arm free.

'Race you home, Nellie,' she called, lolloping sideways down the lane, 'come on, race you, last one in makes the supper.'

Eleanor began to run wildly, heedlessly down the lane.

'No one need know, you know — we shall keep it quiet. I promise to keep my eyes off you in the office, even at lunch — and then we can go away together for week-ends.'

2

Eleanor sat hunched forward in the armchair looking down at Bea who leant against her knees, staring into the fire. Their two pairs of stockings hung smoking over the fireguard, giving off a wet sheep smell. Eleanor saw the office, now a place suffused with meaning. 'Some notes for Miss Carmichael,' she would say, gathering up papers, sweeping down the corridor into Bea's office: 'I have something for you,' and Bea might wonder for a moment – a present, a declaration, a new week-end plan? 'Just notes, my dear, just notes.' And she'd be out again, waving through the glass door, carrying back to her desk the secret of the light in Bea's face as she looked up, the secret of her wide mouth smiling as it smiled at no one else.

She looked down at Bea's hair, laid her hand upon it, it sprang between her fingers – naturally wavy, she thought, didn't need doing – and soft and bright beneath her hand. To lay her hand like this on her lover's head, this head resting so quietly on her right knee, was such a joy. Almost painful, the happiness of this touch that brought her inside Bea's defences – she'd been let in behind them, and her love now flowed straight out through her fingers like electricity. She felt it rushing from her into Bea's head as she stroked the soft hair. To live like this. To live like this, she thought, it's all I want. We can live quietly, in the country perhaps – and to the world we shall be just spinsters, best left alone. But to ourselves, we shall be everything, be open.

She said aloud: 'To each other we can be ourselves, our real selves – that's what matters. So long as we act the same in the office, put on an act for them, who'll care what we do? No one'll notice – who knows what Miss Humbril does at home, I bet you never even thought of it, and all the time she might be hiding a secret lover!'

Bea sighed, 'I don't think so, dear, I think she has an invalid aunt, or something like that – don't you remember last winter she was knitting that pair of bedsocks, "To keep the old lady warm," she kept saying. You're such a romantic, Nellie, you don't know what goes on, half the time – you don't even listen to the gossip, you're too far away. You don't listen at all.'

Bea paused, and began to pick at a fleck of mud on her skirt. 'I don't like secrets,' she said, pecking and pecking at the skirt with her finger-nail, 'why shouldn't people know what I'm doing? I want them to know.' She leant back, finally, and turned to look up at Eleanor: 'But no one must know about us.'

* * * * * * * * * * * * * * *

3

'It's no good, dear, I just can't this week-end.' Bea's shoes scuffed gravel. She dragged one foot, gouging a channel in the path. 'I must go and see my parents, they're expecting me. I promised I'd go — there's a party on.'

They walked round and round the pond. Eleanor hated to meet in Kensington Gardens, everyone else seemed to meet there too, especially in August, and they could all hear, she thought, they could all hear fragments of conversation and wonder at it, and speculate. Even the children seemed to stare knowingly as they passed.

'And I can't come with you.' Eleanor's voice was flat, accusing, though she'd meant it to sound otherwise — for she quite saw that Bea was right, after all, was only being realistic. But almost despite herself she went on, 'You've met my mother.'

'Oh, Nellie, you know that's different, she doesn't think, doesn't question — she accepted me as a pleasant person, as your friend, without a second thought. Simply because you introduced me. But don't you see, my parents aren't like that — they'll want a bracket for you, they'll have to place you somewhere? "Who is this girl?", they'll say to themselves, "What's she for, where does she fit in?" You have to have some position, you see, for they know that you must have some relation to me, some tie.' Bea jammed her fists into her skirt pockets and stood still for a moment, staring down at the gravel. 'And they know I'm too old to have girl-friends.'

She looked up at Eleanor who was staring past her, scowling at a small boy with a dingy red-painted boat who had stopped near them, his head on one side. As he registered Eleanor's scowl he reddened and then bared his teeth in a surprising snarl before turning away down the Broad Walk.

'Ugh, I hate children, their naked interest! ... I feel so crowded in on, suddenly, as if everyone were questioning me — do you know what I mean?'

Eleanor looked quizzically in her turn at Bea, at her skirt with the bright red and yellow stripes going round and round it, at the primrose yellow blouse, the big brooch on the lapel. She didn't look absolutely as if she did know, Eleanor thought, she looked more like this summer's look

4

for the young girl about town in Harper's. But then that was the trouble, and there she was falling into it: there was no way either of them could look like they knew how that felt, or how a whole range of other things felt between them, for that matter.

'Oh, I'm sorry, I know how difficult it is, of course you can't take me with you — I quite see that.'

She plunged on, trying to make amends for her lack of faith, 'It's just that I get lonely by myself here and I wonder what you're doing, and what you're saying, and whether you're having a good time —'

'You don't have to be lonely here, you know,' said Bea, watching her foot digging little heaps and hollows in the gravel. 'You could go out —'

'But I don't want you to feel guilty about going, I want you to tell me about it, that's all.'

'Well, I'll try,' Bea said, setting off round the pond again. 'there isn't much. I'll get home, tomorrow evening, and they'll have waited supper for me. So they can feed me up and ask me silly questions about the office. And then they'll tell me all the local news and especially what's happening next weekend, a party or a fête, there's always something, something for me to come back for. Then there's the questions about my young man, have I been out? Did I go dancing? Who is he? And I'll tell them about Teddy Anderson, and I'll say you and I went out with him and his friend. And my father'll probably say, nice young man that, I liked him — you must bring him down again some time soon, and I'll say, yes of course, he'd love to come again, only it must be after the gymkhana, he can't stand them, says he went to so many as a boy when there was nothing else to do in the country. And that'll let me off for a week or two and then—'

'You mean you're going to take Teddy down again? But don't you think that'll make them think it's serious?'

Bea shrugged vaguely, 'Oh, I don't think so.' She paused. 'I have to take someone down, it may as well be him — he gets on well with the ladies in the tea tent at fêtes and things.'

They walked on round the pond, drawn on round it, following their thoughts faster along the narrow path, the yellow summer grass on one side, on the other the dim water, grey even in the hot evening sunshine. Bea found a kleenex in her pocket and began to shred it, scattering tiny white rags along the path.

'It has to happen some time, you know,' she said.

'Are you going to marry Teddy?' asked Eleanor, stupidly, walking on.

5

'Or someone. It doesn't matter who, you know. It doesn't matter who.'

The phrases came out in bitter spurts, punctuated by little fragments of tissue cast down onto the path. Eleanor stopped then, so suddenly that she almost fell. All at once the ground had opened up — one moment, Bea talking about her week-end — only a week-end, she would be back on Monday. Back for lunches at Lyons and evenings at the pictures. Back for her. To think about, to know. And now here they were at the edge of something, something final. How had it happened? Had she brought it on? Perhaps she shouldn't have bullied about the week-end — she didn't care, Bea could have as many week-ends as she wanted. Why did it have to be like this? But she saw that it was too late to avoid it, now.

'Does it? Does it have to happen some time?' she said at last, hopelessly.

She drew the white cardigan off her arm and began to put it on, doing up the buttons slowly, one by one, starting at the bottom.

'It has to end some time — for you as well. You make it sound like I'm the one that's going off.' Bea bit her lip, and chewed on the remains of the kleenex, 'I'm just facing facts, that's all.'

'But no one has to know,' protested Eleanor, weakly, 'you can go on going to your parents', we can see each other like we do now —'

'No!' Bea burst out as if a dam had crumpled in her head, filling her mind in a great rush with the knowledge she had been keeping back. She had kept it back, making a calm space for herself, where she could meet Eleanor and not think of the future. But now she saw that sooner or later she must succumb to the mass building behind the wall, 'But don't you see, that's just it, no one has to know. No one *does* know. No one *can*. There's no place for it.'

Bea started off round the pond again and then stopped, seeing that Eleanor was still standing, rooted, her cardigan half-buttoned. She came back, took Eleanor's arm. 'Come on,' she said, 'I hate this place too — let's go and get a drink. There's that hotel over the road that's quiet. We can sit down there, out of the way.'

They found a corner hidden from the street, the passers-by. Bea began again — she saw so clearly now how impossible it all was. Eleanor must be made to see too, to accept it. That it had to end.

'It's the secrecy, Nellie, I can't go on with it — and I know you're the same, you want the girls in the office to know, you want my parents to know – but that's impossible; if they knew they wouldn't understand.'

Bea felt that she wasn't at all at the heart of it. But Eleanor had seen, had to take it up. 'Yes,' she said, 'and you can't live a secret, because out in the open you find you're living something else. It's odd, that, isn't it – the secrecy is so exciting in a way, having something that you can't begin to explain to anyone else; and then you realise that there really is no way of explaining it – that it's so totally inexplicable to the rest of the world that it doesn't exist. You can't live it. Everything we do out there denies it. Everything.'

'It's no good being maudlin, there's nothing we can do about it.'

Bea didn't want to go on, beating her down with how things were. I sound so brisk, she thought, and I feel so helpless. She found Eleanor's hand under the table and held it. A pathetic gesture. A stupid inadequate gesture. We should have screams and storms and weeping. But there's no room for that here.

Eleanor's hand was loose in hers, she was leaning back, her face pale against the plush. She muttered, 'I can't seem to think of anything sensible. I keep finding myself wanting to say things I haven't said since I was at school. Stupid, useless things.' She paused. 'It's not fair, it's just not fair.'

They stared at each other for a moment. Then Bea stood up abruptly. 'I'm going to buy some cigarettes. Do you want another drink?' She felt in her pockets, 'I haven't much money, can I borrow some?' Eleanor opened her bag, 'I've only got ten bob,' she said, thrusting the note across the table, 'but you'd better get us both another drink. Adult props, and that. We don't seem to know how to do this at all, do we?'

Bea came back, balancing the glasses, and with two bags of crisps. 'Here are the cigarettes,' she said, feeling into one pocket, 'and I remembered the matches.'

'Crisps! – Bea, you're making this into a treat –'

'I'm not, don't be silly. I was starving, that's all, and there's nothing else unless you go into the dining room. You're being romantic again, Nellie, and it's so useless – can't we eat and be miserable at the same time, can't we have a little fun despite it?'

'It's so difficult altogether,' said Eleanor, accepting her crisps, 'I don't know what we can do or what we can't. I suppose we can do what we like.

7

It's just that I keep feeling like a child — and now here I am sorting through my crisps hoping there'll be two bags of salt.'

She put the crisps down suddenly. 'Give me a cigarette. We can watch to see if my hand trembles.'

She lit a Players and lent back. In the centre of the ceiling a huge fan turned slowly. The cigarette smoke was drawn upwards and towards it. Eleanor inhaled and felt the smoke hit the back of her head, her scalp, felt her limbs loosen and tingle. 'I suppose you want children,' she said. Bea didn't answer. 'Or you'll have them, anyway. What shall you call them? I hope one of the girls is an Eleanor, as a second name at any rate. You could say it was for Eleanor of Aquitaine — though I don't remember much about her, except she was rich. Perhaps I could visit sometimes, the country seat — is there one in Teddy's family, or shall you be only a solicitor's wife? Your brother'll have your father's place, that's how the upper classes order their successions, isn't it? I shall come down and play auntie to the little boys, and if you decide to be open with your new husband I shan't be asked too often, and Teddy will be careful not to leave us alone in the shrubbery.'

'Oh, for god's sake, shut up. You sound like some drawing-room farce. I don't give a damn for all that position, the county lady stuff, having select parties and whom one can invite and going up to town to put things on account —' Bea stopped suddenly — there she was, almost getting carried away by the same catalogue. It was so easy: one knew exactly what it was that that life involved, down to its smallest detail. And if you thought of it for a moment it was like turning on a tap that drowned you in seconds in a rush of inevitable daily life. She tried again to reach the clarity she had had in the park.

'None of that's the point,' she said. 'I could give all that up. But what is there instead? Can you see us, living together somewhere? All the time we'd be thinking, should I have brought her to this? Can she be happy like this? Does she want to get away? And all the time there'd be the men, beckoning, like safe harbours in a storm. A way to get away from all the questions — you don't want to live together, what can you see in each other . . .' Bea's voice trailed off, her hands pleated her skirt.

'It's not recognised, Nellie,' she said at last, despairing of an explanation. 'It's not something that anyone thinks that you do.'

Eleanor lit another Players, carefully, and leaned back once more. 'You needn't go on,' she said. 'I quite understand. It's not your fault, either. I'm not blaming you, at all.'

They sat in silence; after a while Bea lit herself a cigarette. Eleanor stood up, 'I'm going home now, I think. I'll leave you my crisps.' She gathered up her handbag, found her sandals under the table and walked away, her steps soundless on the thick carpet. But at the entrance she turned and came back. 'I want you to remember that it just happened. It just appeared between us both — spontaneously.' She turned back to the street.

Eleanor had left the cigarettes. There were seven, which Bea smoked. When it was growing dark outside and men carrying whiskeys had begun to nose out her hiding place, Bea left the hotel and, finding that she had kept Eleanor's change, took a bus home.

* * * * * * * * * * * * * *

Bea lifted the flap of the tent and stood out in the sunshine. A cigarette now. At breakfast, lighting up. So much to be drawn in, sent out with the smoke, ordered. The shopping list, the girls' things to take, buns into a tin. So much for that. Tim, then. Eyeing her over his teacup, putting it down. The tension hitting, a second before the silence was broken. Not a peaceful lull, this: order the day in your mind. Thin, edgy calm before the storm. Tim putting down his teacup.

'I do wish you'd give them up, dear – such a horrible habit, and I can't see that you need them – for stress, or anything.'

Bea felt her daughters stiffen, twitch as they caught the scent of the cloud of irritation rolling across the table at her, catching them in its eddies, large and blundering and indiscriminate as it rolled out. Ginny and Nell fidgeted, they must get away. Didn't want it hanging over them, ruining their fête. Why did it have to be this morning, couldn't they quarrel some other time? Nell spooned her cereal faster, grimaced at Ginny across the table. Ginny put back her piece of toast – but that was no good; he saw, and saw them trying to get away. It fed Mr Lloyd's ill-temper, that his daughter should accusingly put back her slice of toast; a perfectly sensible suggestion – and here they were acting as if he were bullying them.

'Eat the toast now you've fingered it, Ginny,' he said, and glared down the table at Bea.

Smoking, she sensed her daughters' anger turned on her – couldn't she avoid annoying him, couldn't she smoke somewhere else, why did she have to go ruining their morning?

'You'd better go and get ready, if you've finished your breakfasts,' she said, 'we'll have to go quite soon to see to the tea-tent.' Trying to keep an edge from her voice, calling a truce between them – or they'd pay her out. Wouldn't fetch things, be clumsy with the cakes, rude to the old ladies.

'One must have one's vices,' said Bea, lightly.

But that wasn't enough, couldn't be enough, for hadn't she got the girls on her side, ganging them up against him? They'd grow up without principle, siding with their mother all the time, taking the easy way out, smoking, doing just as they pleased.

'I don't see why,' Tim said, 'that's just one of those things people say. Means nothing. Vices are to be avoided, obviously. You'll be telling the girls they can do what they like, next — they're getting to that age.' He had worked himself into a rage, seeing it all, suddenly, the whole picture — his daughters brought up all wrong, turning out loose women at the mercy of every passing fancy. 'They'll be coming across all kinds of temptations — and what will you say? "one must have one's little vices".'

Bea waited, trying not to listen to the detail. Not now, she thought, not now. I've too much to do. So I'm not bringing them up properly.

'I think they listen to you more than to me, dear, on the whole.'

'I set them a better example, certainly,' he said, noticing out of the window that the honeysuckle was coming on to bloom. It would need to be staked up against the wall again. 'Hadn't you better be going?' he said, folding the paper.

Bea put her hand out to a rope, the cigarette was making her dizzy. She'd have to eat some of those stolid cakes, not done to eat your own. Ginny coming up to her, behind the tea urn, wanting to know which were their buns.

'But we must eat someone else's, dear.'

And then Nell had come along and Ginny was hissing at her, 'We mustn't eat our own buns! We mustn't!' 'Cannibalism,' Nell had said, and they were off round the tables teasing the old ladies. 'You mustn't eat your own cakes, you know, it's cannibalism — your own flesh and blood!'

Bea looked across the lawn, down to the roped-off square at the bottom of the slope where the exhibitions were to be held. The primary school's gym display first of all, Ginny was in that, of course. She'd gone down half-an-hour ago in her yellow aertex shirt and her blue pants to help put up the apparatus — there was a crowd of them down there now, little girls with bodies in three segments, like ants, a blue, a bright yellow, a brown head. They looked colourful and cheerful in the distance. Tea wouldn't start for an hour or so — Bea decided to go down and watch the gymnastics.

A few chairs had been placed in front for the old men and their wives. The rest of the crowd, women, children, many of them in costume for the dancing display or still wearing some of their fancy dress, milled about. A knot of women, mothers of Ginny's friends, were glued together by the crush, far across the lawn. They waved vaguely. Children kept coming to stand in front of the chairs, blocking the old people's view. Each time an old man in a pork pie hat would put out his walking stick and poke at them, calling 'Clear a way there, clear a way!' And then his wife would lean over to him, knotting her headscarf, whispering, 'You mustn't do that, dear.' And mothers in the crowd would call their children away, to them; but always new ones took their places in front of the old man's chair. Bea stood behind a clump of other women, strangers, talking amongst themselves.

Close up the girls in their games clothes were distinct from one another. Their hair cleared to different shades, even their shirts a range of yellows. Ginny's shirt was bright primrose, shining in the middle of the line waiting to start — she would put on her new shirt for the display. The identical costume, now that you were close, showed up each child's faults: that one had knock-knees, at the back; one next to Ginny, perhaps she was older than the others, stood a head taller and carried her shoulders hunched, cupped round her chest. They all looked odd, imperfect somehow, lined up like that, thought Bea, lined up in that uniform they looked like a class of misfits on display. Ginny wasn't ever very gainly, but now she looked like a stick insect. For a moment Bea stared at the line, a rack of specimens — weren't they going to start, did they all have to stand there looking at them? And then the woman standing at the horse called to them, put a whistle between her teeth and they began, running up one by one, grasping handles and vaulting, some doing handstands in the air and having to be caught — that was where they'd put Elsa, the fat one, catching her classmates as they turned through the air — her blotchy legs reddening as more and more came over the horse to fall into her arms. Bea watched Ginny come somersaulting over in a great rush — surely she was going to land on her back — and then Elsa's big hands reached out, twitched the flying body round, and Ginny landed on her feet, rocked for a second, her knees sagging under the impact, and then bounced away. The display was short, and the girls were dissecting the apparatus and carrying pieces away, one at each corner. Like ants taking away sugar, thought Bea, watching the teacher. Her arms folded, whistle between her teeth, feet apart but grinning at the girls as they tried to run with their loads, at their parody of discipline as they giggled and heaved. All at once it looked like a riot — there were twenty of them clustered round the biggest horse, shrieking and shoving — and then she had marched in, dropped her whistle from her mouth, was issuing instructions, had picked up one end, and the horse was carried off the field.

Well, she can deal with them, thought Bea, and they produce jumps and vaults for her. For her, Ginny isn't the one with the stick legs, Ginny is Ginny who likes to do the newest vaults and is a little reckless and doesn't like to be caught. That's all right — Bea hardly knew what she was reassuring herself about. The girls had fun, and they liked showing off to everyone at the fête, gave them a sense of achievement — so what was the matter? It was those stick legs — everyone seeing her daughter in a line — the one with the knock-knees, the one with the stick legs.

There was a lull now and she could hear the women in front of her.

'Yes, that's Beverly Tanner's daughter, outgrown her strength, I'd say.'

'Don't teach posture at school any more, do they — there used to be prizes for it.' And they laughed.

'I suppose this gym is instead of the tap dancing they used to have. It's a change, they used to look so nice in their black and white frocks.'

Bea stood listening, she hung on their words; waiting for a clue. How was it, how had it seemed to them, was it all right? They were older, no daughters of theirs in the display; to them it was just part of the day, the ordinary pattern of the fête. One year tap dancing, the next gym, all the same. But Bea stayed in her place. Something was happening next — what was it? She ought to get back to the tea tent, but what was happening next? It was the dancing school, it began suddenly — some tinsel music screeching out of the loudspeaker, a tune she vaguely remembered from somewhere, was it children's parties? and the dancing. Little girls in batches, costumed as stars or rainbows, singing nursery rhymes; older ones in tutus or leotards performing ballet steps, in pinafores, in little skirts, in ankle socks, with ribbons in their hair, with their legs bare. Bea stood rigid. In front of her the women hummed and murmured, 'Aren't they sweet?' and clapped loudly, encouragingly, after each piece. But Bea could not listen to them; she stood rigid with horror watching the little girls cavorting desperately in front of her, forgetting their words, their eyes searching out their teacher who waved and gesticulated and mouthed, urging them on at the side of the grass. Bea saw their small bodies decked out, to be judged, laughed at, found wanting. It was a horrible sight. The old man in the hat said suddenly, 'My, look at them fat little legs!' Bea tore herself away and plunged off up the hill to the tent.

* * * * * * * * * * * * * *

13

Bea lay in bed, hearing through the wall — thin, and soggy as if it might be cardboard — Nell and Ginny shifting in their narrow bunks next door. On the other side of the room the window glimmered; the sea still held a faint light, vague and diffuse, drawn from the half-hidden moon or held back perhaps from the brilliance of the day. Bea's skin burned quietly hot beneath sheets that smelt of gorse and salt.

It was pleasant to lie freely, she thought, without anyone. Without Tim, in this narrow bed. She listened for sounds stilll, through the wall. But how could he have left her here, alone with the children? Didn't he realise? She couldn't keep it up by herself. There was no structure, nothing behind. Tim was its flesh. The normality of the world. She needed him there. Without him, it seemed to vanish; slowly, lingering like ectoplasm draining from a seance. Odd disconnected limbs, floating for a moment in the air. Gradually she no longer knew why she was being this thing, their mother. Carrying out her part. Thrusting at them — theirs. Something had exposed arbitrariness, bleached flesh from bones. It had begun to seem ridiculous. Why must one wash, have supper? Why this? Why now? Why at all? She had found she did not know. There were no reasons for things. But it had somehow to go on. The eating, sleeping, washing. Somehow, she went on pushing on through the routine. How much heavier it seemed, the ordinary domestic burden. And the meaninglessness ate at what held the children to her. She could feel no rights. If they chose to exclude her, she could only acquiesce. And there was nowhere to go. She would be left, suddenly adrift on her beach towel while they schemed behind rocks. Left staring at an azure sky, their lunch drying in the sand beside her.

Bea watched her thoughts running restlessly, felt some urgency invade her body. Not just to lie here like this, doing nothing, mind racing. Get up then, get up. I must have movement, she thought. No sound came through the wall. She got out of bed and dressed, groping for cigarettes on the bedside table.

She found a pencil and a scribbling block in the kitchen. 'I have gone for a walk and will be back soon.' She stared at the message for a moment. There seemed nothing else.

14

The tide was out and the beach, its dark sand, welcoming. Bea took the cliff path, feeling her way in the semi-darkness. Her mind slowed to the rhythm of her feet on the rough steps. She walked slowly towards the sea and then steadily along by its edge, her stride lengthening. The sea, quiet at the tide's turning, pounded only dimly. I am not free, thought Bea. She was on parole only, the children sleeping sentries in their bunks, their very carelessness the greater tie. She could not rid herself of them, even now when the weave of routine seemed loosened. Through all that some tangible link dragged her on, her alone. I am not free.

Bea stopped to light a cigarette; and remembered Eleanor, walking Devon sands ten years ago. It was Eleanor in the hotel that she remembered, drawling out that cameo sketch of Bea's life, her easy life. Her safety among the county middle classes. It had come back before: as if from a distance, hearing Eleanor's voice in her ear, seeing her ironic smile. When Nell was born, it had been there again, in the background. Was that why she had argued and held out to name the child? Fighting the battle for it with a strange excitement until it had become a necessity for her. Tim could only give way, humorous before her passion. And once she had won, she had almost hated him for acquiescing. For binding her. For she found that she had not rid herself of that vision. She stood still now on the sands. More often, after that, her daily life came to her — as she sat over breakfast, as she walked vaguely in the garden after lunch, as she wrote shopping lists, as she put down the 'phone — her life came before her as an extension of Eleanor's description in that hotel lounge. A voice in her head spoke quiet disdain.

And yet why had this stupid sneer such power, that it sat on her shoulder, pouncing on the trivia of her life, shredding and spitting and jeering on the edge of her mind? Bea stood, one foot fidgeting with the sand. It was ridiculous that she could not get free; she did not feel herself that caricature, for whom meaning lay in delicate china, the proprieties of life. She was other than that. She was thirty-five, and she went for walks in the night on dark beaches and smoked too many cigarettes. And because she did do some of the things that Eleanor's ghost laughed at, she knew that that stupid caricature described more than insensitivity, propriety, blindness. There was worth in her life. In these lives around her. Worth that made such little rituals irrelevant.

How often before she had fought this same battle with Eleanor's contempt, wormed out the foolishness of Eleanor's ignorant dismissal. And still that casual, careless denial hit her. Now as she walked on across the sand Eleanor stalked beside her, dark and leaning over her.

'I saw how it would be,' she was saying, 'where has it got you? What are you now Bea? What will you be soon?'

The endless accusing litany went on, her life strung out flat, a long featureless expanse to be walked from end to end through unchanging landscape, steps becoming more difficult each day, the vista narrowing or widening, no matter, all out of reach.

'Be quiet, you're an outdated symbol, that's all!' Bea shouted at last. The cliffs echoed faintly. She looked around: there was no one in sight.

'Well,' she muttered softly, 'you had nothing else to offer — what alternatives are there? I can't see that there are any.'

'Of course not,' retorted Eleanor, striding on down the beach, almost too fast for Bea — it seemed as if she, this shade, were more full of life than Bea and threatened to outstrip her — 'you can't imagine anything other than your current life, your current choices, your current expectations. That's because of the life you lead. It curtails your vision.'

And the wraith dematerialised and would say no more, go no further; the life it might be leading was beyond Bea's imagination, she could not see it. She could not see what she herself could be doing in that thing's company. But she could not ignore that flat ironic voice: it held within it her belief in the existence of possibilities that she could not now encompass; she clutched at that thin voice, fed it, worried it, and hoped that it would still somehow mysteriously bloom.

She felt relief, as if a weight had lifted for a moment, as she climbed the path back to the cottage. Outside the gate she paused to watch the darkness cut by the moon, free now of clouds, as it set over the sea. It was a fine holiday place, she thought, you can do what you want here, once you know. Why shouldn't she let the girls do as they liked, let herself do as she liked? Nothing need fall apart.

'At least,' she said aloud, turning in at the gateway, 'I didn't marry Teddy Anderson.'

* * * * * * * * * * * * * * *

16

It was in August that Tim Lloyd travelled down to join his wife and daughters for a week. As he drove he thought of cold rugged places: on the slopes every day, swooping down from the highest reaches, almost inaccessible pinnacles, crossing brilliant snow at speed, silently.

At the top of the cliff Tim sat in the parked car staring out with mild surprise over the bay, content to remain inert in the warm evening sunshine and to watch a few sailing boats far out on the water tacking this way and that. Other people's holidays, he thought, climbing reluctantly out of the car. As he walked down the path large straggling families passed him on their way up, decked with towels and buckets, carrying sandals and footballs and small tired hiccuping children with reddened faces. There seemed to be an unending stream of them, calling noisily to each other, urging on children who dawdled or cried at the sight of the hill still to be climbed; they passed in a steady procession and they looked strangely at Tim, who still wore his city suit.

He found Bea and the children out in the patch of garden, stooped over a butterfly.

'It's a Holly Blue, a Holly Blue,' Nell was saying, 'I looked it up.'

'It's very dark for one of those,' Ginny said, 'look, it's darker than navy, much darker than the picture.'

Bea looked up as Tim opened the gate. 'Hello,' she called, 'do you know whether this is a Holly Blue? Ginny says it's the wrong colour.'

'And too late in the year,' added Ginny.

They all straightened and stood aside a little. Tim moved in to peer down at the butterfly.

'Oh yes. A Holly Blue.'

Suddenly he reached forward and in a moment his cupped hands held the butterfly.

'You've caught it — won't it squash?'

Nell pried open his fingers: in the dark cavern of his hands she could see the butterfly crawling about, flapping its wings.

'It won't hurt it,' Tim said, 'if you catch it like this and then hold it for a while, it'll stay on your palm when you open your hands — see?'

And he opened out his hands and the butterfly paused, quiet, on his finger for a moment before flying off over the gate. Nell and Ginny began to run about on the path outside, looking for butterflies to catch. Tim and Bea turned indoors. He should have come before, Bea thought.

Bea had in her mind a list of the houses and gardens to which they would go while Tim was down. And then there was the beach to be walked, rewarding in both directions. On his first morning they set out to walk east along the beach; the tide would be going out as they walked and they could have lunch at the next village in the bay. Nell and Ginny had to keep further away from the sea than usual because they were wearing shoes, for the lunch, and so they turned cartwheels and called Tim loudly, showing him shells and interesting marbled stones. They felt complete, things were as they should be, and they were going out to lunch.

Bea stared at the sea, the cliffs, the sand. They seemed to her beautiful, and by that she meant that they seemed moving, poignant, as she looked at them. Or perhaps it was her own inability to describe the scene, or her feeling for it, that held her? She glanced inland a little to where groups of people played games in the sand, the stretch of sand so broad at the ebb that they were at some distance. Occasionally a trickle would detach itself from the crowd and wind down to the sea, carrying balls, wearing rubber rings, to jump in the surf. Bea did not like to see them, wished that mist would fall daily and rain drive them away. They seemed careless of the sea's peace. She felt the landscape, the beauty she saw in it to be fragile, that it would not survive these callous excursions upon its delicate wet sands, its gorse hills. I cannot bear to see people here, she thought, I am afraid. She could not live here, though it was so beautiful, she would have to live somewhere where people did not go.

Ginny was bending over something at the very edge of the tide. It was a crab, lying inert in the sand. It had two legs missing on one side, but when she bent close Bea saw that it was alive, its eyes swivelling.

'I wonder what it's doing here,' she said, fearing that it could only be about to die, beached up like this, and lethargic. Tim came up.

'My, an edible crab! I didn't know it was the season,' and he stooped and picked up the crab by its shell. The crab's legs waved vaguely and Nell shrieked.

'We can have it for supper — delicious with mayonnaise.'

He had the crab by the pincers, swung it in the air, exposing its under-belly. Bea watched the claws waving.

18

'We can't take it into the hotel for lunch.'

'Well then, we can take it home now and have it for lunch instead. Crab meat is a rare delicacy,' he added to the girls.

'I want lunch in a hotel,' Nell said.

'And so do I, Tim — you don't realise we haven't eaten out at all while we've been here, it'll be a wonderful change.' Bea hung on his arm, 'We can pick it up on our way back.'

'All right. But I should have thought crab would be enough of a change.'

They moved on down the beach, Nell and Ginny running ahead. The crab lay where Tim had dropped it in the sand.

* * * * * * * * * * * * * * * *

'We must have been crazy to come here,' Ann said.

She pulled the plug in the sink, turned her back, wiped her hands on her trousers.

'You said that already.'

Dee got up from the table and leaned against it. She lit a cigarette from the packet in her breast pocket, 'I think that if you want to go back to town you should go. I don't want to be in the position of keeping you here. But you know all that.'

'Yes, I know all that. So we needn't go on saying it to each other. Or, if we could stop saying it to each other for a moment, perhaps we wouldn't need to say it.' I have begun all wrong, Ann realised, she thinks I'm blaming her for bringing us here together, to this. That I want to leave. Fracture is easy. And so now they must go back to common ground quickly, into the gentle shorthand of reassurance. Reassert their understanding, the ease of it. And more than that, more than well-rehearsed phrases, some new fragile communication. And then go on. She could not let herself think about all that had to be done, could only begin.

'We came here partly to make a tangible commitment,' Ann said. 'So that we could believe in it. Because it was always so destructive, or time-consuming, to have to be doubting and reaffirming all the time.'

'Well, it was also experimental, for me anyway. To see whether the commitment could be positive itself. It wasn't just a question of getting it out of the way, like signing a declaration and taking it for granted from then on as if we were married. We were going to work on it, I thought.' Ann always made it sound as if that's what they were doing, some pathetic replica of marriage, Dee thought. She's afraid of being trapped, though she can't say so, only that she might have had qualms once, in the past and put them behind her.

Dee was angry as she watched Ann backed up against the draining board, her knuckles round the edge, already as if she were in the firing line, hounded. I am to be blamed, she thought, because she has upset me, because I have allowed myself to be upset. I am to feel guilty for being angry in my turn. She let the thoughts run: did Ann think that she was the only one who wanted something better? She was tired of pouring her love and trust and thought into this and getting in return suspicion. There were other things to do, no need to waste time. I don't have to hang on, she thought.

'It hasn't entirely worked for me,' she said.

Further in, into the slide, further apart. Another opportunity for cut and run — say that Dee has brought it on, Ann thought, blame her. Not to fool myself, but to make it easier. There's no turning this aside now, it's here, full-scale: sometimes the breach is closed, right words at the right time, physical gesture; only a postponement, though, and it'll come out again, dragging on. Better to go on through.

Freedom, leaving, the new image wan and alone, the pleasures of grief. In a second these same fantasies come, fleshed out, vibrant with a full range of emotions. I don't want anything to do with that, do I? Not leaving again. I have things to do here, I shouldn't forget. Ann moved over to the table.

'I think it's been harder for you in a way. I'm used to this, done it before.'

'And always left it.'

Ann's hand clenched on the tea-pot. She got up again, took two mugs from the draining board, bent into the refrigerator for milk. Why was it Dee had always to be searching through what she said, not taking the intention, looking for loopholes, accusing her of fluency? A crime to have lived always with other women, a crime to be able to speak about it.

That's not what I meant,' she said. 'Yes, I left — but not because of the demands living together makes on you. I'm saying that maybe you find that harder than you expected. I can do that bit, switch off when I need to read and work, I'm good at being ruthless and selfish when I've had enough. I take care of myself.' If it goes so against the grain, why the hell do we do it, Ann thought. Another challenge for puritans. And I get shit for having learnt self-preservation.

'I do find that difficult, yes. And I want it to be easy, being alone. Like waking alone in my own room used to be easy. But we're not talking about what matters, about what there is.' Enough of all this unreality. What they had managed didn't amount to anything. We are nowhere, Dee thought. The new ground hadn't been broken. A few scratches here and there.

'It's very important to me,' she said, 'trying to do this, build some kind of real intimacy. I don't want it to fail. I don't want it to fail for some small lack of effort in a particular area. I won't give up easily, but I don't think we're getting anywhere.'

Ann didn't know, she knew, where they might be going. But the threat of Dee's absence reminded her — of what she wanted, or what she called what she wanted, not knowing either what it would be like if they made it. But still it brought up a physical longing for those possibilities, adrenalin as if they could get there by climbing, excitement at the vastness of the task. It was hard to remember what moments when they had been further on had been like: the physical images might remain, but those movements had been made so often also without the same feeling; of the feeling itself only a suggestion, she knew it had been encompassing, a sense of enduring perception — but of what. It seemed more fragile as she thought. And what was it worth if the sense of enduring faded? But it need not fade; one must try to get somewhere.

'I want to go on. I think we are learning, are nearer.'

'Then why did you say we were crazy to come here?'

'Because of the isolation. The complete lack of support — you know. We fight different battles out here, but they still take energy, and we don't get any back from other women because there are none. Look, if I want to go back to the city it's not you I want to leave, it's this desert. I'm tired of always having to use cactus skills, as if that's all there ever was for lesbians in the world — drink in the fleeting support of the ghetto, grow a thick skin to withstand the heat of a hostile environment, go sit in the desert for a year drinking your juices meanly.'

Dee had moved through to the other room, to the fire. Ann shouted through while she stayed to pour more tea, rushing off gladly on this tide of metaphor, less escape than rest. A lull and only a lull, she thought; nothing that can turn into a way out, too edgy and watchful for that, 'I want to be a lush thick-petalled stinking ghetto flower loosing my scent thick on the tropical night.' She came through with her cup and paused in the doorway, 'I can't really pretend I like the idea, though. I'd rather be something much more contained. Small climbing and scentless, perhaps.'

Dee stared at the rug. A hideous rug, a mess of purple and yellow and with sticky tufts, a classic rented house rug, something no one would want with them, at home. Who could have bought it? A homeless rug. Of course they had to be cacti, but not just out here, where what they were was unrecognised. In the city it was the same, it could not be any different, Ann knew that. So what she was wanting was the other women, and

22

whether they went back together or not the result would be the same.

'I need them too, you know,' Dee said, 'but I'm afraid that what I want from them is not the same as what you want.' And out of the dreariness, there really was no future in it, she said, 'Of course that is what you are, a lush flower.'

'Dee, what I want from them is a community, a sense of political significance, group security, perhaps solidarity and identity if that's possible — not something personal. All I am saying is that we can't live out here as we would want to live because out here we aren't what we want to be. We need the dimension that only being part of them provides, the political dimension, if we are to be who we want to be.'

They sat next to each other on the rug, facing the fire. Dee leaned wearily into Ann's shoulder.

'I know all that.'

* * * * * * * * * * * * * * *

'Bacon hotpot, sounds horrible, doesn't it? But I love it,' she saw that she had her friend's attention, 'a layer of potatoes, a layer of onion, a layer of bacon, a layer of potatoes,' her eyes moved gradually to the ceiling, 'and I make a white sauce with it, for the vegetables.' The two women at the table paused to sip their drinks, considering this recipe, would it work with streaky or did it have to be back? At the next table Dee stored it away, seeing as she did so a number of problems that she too should be able to solve internally without fear: to guess at whether you would need to add liquid, how fast it should cook, for how long.

A boy came into the bar. He bought his pint and stood next to the two women's table. Eva refocused her gaze.

'Hello Paul,' she said, 'and how's the farm?'

'Not too bad.'

'Are you going to join in our darts match?'

'We could do with some young blood, liven us old things up.'

'He won't want to play with us, will you Paul. You'll want to be off with your girlfriend.'

'He should be chivalrous, give us the benefit of his skill for an evening — how about it, Paul?'

'It's no good, Julie, he wants to be with his own — did you want to be with our age when you were his? We must seem ancient to you, Paul.'

'Not really.' Paul grinned, 'Give it a couple more children.'

'I have enough of those —'

'I'm getting on myself — eighteen, nearly past it.'

'I'm old enough to be your mother.'

'Are you really? You're not!'

'Thirty-five. Not giving that away to anyone else — never get anyone onto the darts team.'

There was a long queue in the butcher's. It was the day the fresh poultry came, for the woman at the head of the line was waiting while the head and feet were cut off her chicken and the severed bones roped into its sides. The carcass hit the table with a wet slap, was parcelled up; the butcher's eyes turned to the next in the queue, he called through to the back, 'Mrs Edison's chicken!' and the boy brought out another bird, grasping it around the legs. He swung it up onto the table. 'Legs off?' the butcher enquired, raising his cleaver.

'That's right,' Mrs Edison nodded encouragingly, 'and I'll have the head off wrapped separate.'

'Dog likes it, does he?' said the butcher.

'Parrot,' said Mrs Edison.

In the queue, Dee decided to buy bacon.

The woman in the greengrocer's was polishing apples, two dusters hung from her nylon overalls' pocket. Dee watched from the doorway as she built a sloping wall of fruit at the back of the shop. In the green light of the shop it glistened. The woman stood back, ran her hands through her hair, and grunted. Then she turned towards the door, reaching under a duster for her cigarettes.

'That looks nice,' Dee nodded at the piled apples. The woman stopped short, 'I didn't see you — was going to have a smoke outside.' She put the packet back in her pocket, 'What'll you have?'

'I'm sorry to be in your way.'

The woman turned round from the racks of paper bags, 'If I don't sell some of this, there'll be no money for cigarettes. What's it I can do for you?'

Dee bought potatoes and onons. And then she was caught again by the apples glinting quietly at the back, 'May I have some of those — you needn't take them from the wall, the display, I mean —'

'Unless I do, you won't get any.' The woman faced Dee again, 'That's all there are.'

Dee stared down at her shopping bag. Trying to be thoughtful and they use it to be sharp. There's no getting past any of them. She took the bag of apples, desperately she said, 'And I'll have a bunch of grapes.' She scooped the money out of her pocket, eyed it, 'Just a small one, please.'

The woman came over, the grapes wrapped in tissue paper, saw Dee fiddling with silver, searching all her pockets. 'This is just over six ounces,' she said, 'that do?' She glanced out of the window as she chose a small bag. 'Another load of poultry arrived at the butcher's, I see — always the same huge hens, as if we all had an army to feed,' and she laid the grapes on top of the basket.

Dee turned to leave, and saw the notice pinned to the door frame. She stopped for a second and then walked on out, aware of the woman behind her. Just past the window she stopped again, gazed blankly into the Post

Office. Work mornings in that shop. Might be an idea, to get them off her back. Lab technicians shouldn't go and live in the country, where there isn't any work for them — like draft-resisting, anti-social. They could suddenly refuse to give her any money at all. That or a typing course. Knew how to type already, but you don't admit that. Maybe you can fail typing courses. There were women in the city who'd tried that kind of thing, they'd had to give them up. But that was the city, here they probably never gave up — force you into a job or cut you off.

The form letters, the interviews, the times when no money arrived. Inconvenience always threatening to turn into planned harassment. Dee knew she was weakening, had started to read the magazines again in the library, had tried to find something in those appointment columns that was perhaps only a little different. The salaries calling up small metal fantasies: the weight of a camera body, the shine of chrome. Knowing each job as always the same for her, a place of alienation. Working where she worked against herself, using their methods that she knew as the methods of her extinction. Working a frozen body, warmth around the edges to give the appearance of life, the rest hidden. How show them anything when it was all one, all of her set dead against them. Yet she had sat in the library and felt close again that old chain of necessity that had kept her hanging on to her job, her only respectability. It beckoned from the magazine, so tempting; necessity and luxury.

Well, necessity could be redefined. Here was a job. Dee stared through the Post Office window. A poster advertised a new set of stamps. It wouldn't take all her time or demand that she give herself up. Perhaps it would be a way of getting to know the women in the village. Conversation over the paper bags, perhaps it would lead somewhere.

Dee turned in at the entrance; the woman paused, a broom in her hands.

'Hello — forget something?'

Dee stayed in the doorway for a moment — but the light was behind her, she would want to be able to see her. She stepped forward.

'Not exactly. I saw the advert for a part-time job here — and I wanted to apply.'

'I see.'

The woman leant on her broom, her head on one side, looking at Dee. What was she looking at, Dee wondered. Or was this just to indicate that their relationship had changed, that she was no longer customer but employee; to make clear that this woman now had the right to look her up and down, in silence. She doesn't like me, Dee thought. Perhaps she's annoyed, was hoping someone she thought she could talk to would take the job. Someone her own age. She doesn't think I know enough. Dee saw that beneath the shapeless overall, hanging open, the woman wore baggy brown corduroy trousers, a brown sweater. She was tall, hadn't had to take the hem of her jeans up, and the cord hung limply in folds — tall and thin.

'Are you strong?'

Dee wanted to leave the shop. She didn't want to answer — say 'No' and let her get away with this way of saying she didn't want a woman, they were no use with the crates, or else rant on about strength and stamina, we are stronger than we know. And karate classes, that wouldn't get her the job either.

'I can lift boxes.'

The other woman suddenly grinned, 'I should hope so!' She swung her broom round and began to sweep the back of the shop. 'Why d'you want to work here — rather than anywhere else?' She swept fast, expertly, with energy.

'I need a part-time job.' But if she didn't say more she might as well be in a lab, behind that wall of trivia. Make the risk now, start it at any rate, 'And I wanted if possible to work with some of the local women, maybe get to know them. We're still quite new here.' Dee listened to herself, she sounded suppliant. 'And you sell good fruit. I like that.'

The other woman took her up, 'You're a connoisseur?'

'As much as I need to be.' She took that in silence, went on sweeping, her back still turned.

'You can have the job if you want it — though you may only meet me. Hours are 8.30 'til lunch. Will you start tomorrow?'

Dee nodded and backed out of the shop, smiling. At the corner she turned back for a moment; the woman stood in the doorway, looking after her.

Dee found herself walking home quickly, her head bent to watch her feet as they came down, turned slightly inwards. She slowed and began to look at the hedgerow, the campions shocking pink, the insane yellow of the kingcups. Now that she looked at it, had brought herself out of her thoughts to look, the beauty of the wild flowers was quite startling. She stood still — but could not stay, her mind ranging away at once, crowding with too much else. She walked on, swinging her basket, glancing from side to side; there was so much that she would have to miss.

When she came in through the kitchen door Ann had the door of the fridge open, a cider bottle in her hand.

'Secret drinking, now?'

'Yes, Harold, when you go out to work I take the sherry out from behind the sofa cushions.'

'Destroying my happy home with your vice. Now I need a drink.'

'Here, it's a bit flat. I suppose that's a role not in the best of taste — think of those women really driven to drink, to scheming over the vodka and the housekeeping.'

'No doubt if we'd gone on she would've got the upper hand. You know how we do.'

'No rest, is there? One has to have a feminist fantasy life.' Ann peered into the shopping basket. 'I suppose I do expect correctness of my fantasies — not that they are, I just feel guilty about it.'

'I don't.' Dee sat on the kitchen table, her legs swinging, 'I don't believe in being moral about my fantasies. Of course when they are feminist, it's more exciting.' She grinned over at Ann holding the stalk of grapes under the tap.

Ann came over to the table with the grapes, fitted herself between Dee's knees, 'I know. Your so called feminist fantasies are all about you as an invincible bank robber tough scientist of the new way forward — you and some other lush passionate karate expert.' She steadied herself with a hand on Dee's thigh, arched her back to hold the grapes up over her mouth, 'We can't afford grapes. Who d'you have in mind as the karate expert at the moment?'

'I don't, I stay solitary. The grapes are to celebrate something — are you going to eat them all now?'

'This job of yours makes me nervous.' Ann pushed her plate away and took a cigarette. 'You realise that, don't you.'

'It shouldn't, I don't think.' Dee collected plates together.

'No? As I see it this job means that you've made a commitment to staying here for some time to come. Which makes any attempt to reach some sort of mutual decision about what we're doing rather pointless. I just have to wait about until you've finished it.'

Ann twisted sideways in her chair; out of the window the evening sun illuminated the canes set up for runner beans. 'Those beans went in too early.' She got up from the table abruptly and crossed over to the window; the slanting light caught the leaves in the garden from underneath — it gave them a wilted, flaccid look. Ann leaned her elbows on the sill, 'Maybe we should stop planting things,' she said.

But she felt Dee's arms encircle her, scattering the misery she had begun to build. She could not stare on out at the vegetables, refusing this comfort; she turned round.

'It's not that sort of job,' Dee said. 'When we decide to leave here, I'll give a week's notice. You don't have your identity wrapped in it, like if I were still trying to be professional.'

'You're right, I suppose.' It would give her mornings by herself, vague slow mornings for doing nothing, or for reading science fiction without being seen, or for making drawings with no one to wonder whether anything had been produced. Ann grinned, 'I think I'd have been worried in case she didn't give me the job — and there isn't another greengrocer's. How would you have shopped there?'

Dee was putting the kettle on, 'It wasn't quite as personal as that,' she called, 'she could have said she wanted someone older or more permanent or experienced, or something.'

'But you would have suspected.'

'We suspect that anyway.'

* * * * * * * * * * * * * * * *

Eleanor could not find the right place to walk. She could not sit on the benches overlooking the formal garden: from there she had to watch scores of families strolling on the gravel between the bright lines of flowers; dozens of parents, with their children, walking somehow as if they came here every Sunday, as if they were part of the scene, and belonged to it. Sitting on a bench Eleanor felt that she had momentarily caught a glimpse of a world that continued somewhere else, that normally she did not have access to. These people, in shirt-sleeves and bending to give their small children ice-cream cornets, knew how to behave on a Sunday afternoon. They took for granted, Eleanor realised, their weekly outing to the park if it were fine — just as they took each other for granted, their husbands, their wives, their children. They came to the park and found each other there, confirming the rightness of it all. Eleanor could not stay on her bench, it was too shocking, that this normality was going on in the park and that she had somehow slipped so far away that she had not known it was there. She found a wooded path and at the end of it an unoccupied seat. But she could not forget the families walking among the rose beds and the others, the other people on the benches: a few old couples sharing out papers and sandwiches, an old man huddled over a stick, two men talking to each other in Greek, perhaps, and staring out over the garden, and herself. She did not want to be on that side of the line, one of the bystanders; life was going on down there amongst the roses. Eleanor knew, brought up against these families, that she was being unreasonable and stupid, that she was not doing herself any good; everyone else brought it off, why didn't she? They at least tried to bring it off; and she knew she could manage it if she tried — she should settle for one of them, settle for something. She felt proud and contrary, realising that others had done so, that she was holding herself apart as if she were somebody special. Bea had settled; so what was she waiting for?

Eleanor got up from her bench and began to pace the path, frowning at her feet — there were grass stains on her white sandals. It was not that she was waiting for anything. She had been in love with men before, she had been in love with Bea; it wasn't that she was waiting for that to happen again. She didn't expect that it would. It was that the time with Bea had been as if there had been a lightening of some fog round her mind, as if she could see further —just enough to see how much lay out of reach, that she had not known was there. It had been like the beginning of something, some task that she had found she wanted more than anything to accomplish — that was not quite how it had been, rather she had wanted to do, to live, that task — and now the way was blocked. Well, so it was blocked. But she did not, she did not want to start off on something else — she couldn't make those families in the rose garden her direction any more. Eleanor slumped back onto her bench. You're an incurable fool, she thought, pretending to make up your mind to something and having no idea what it is you're doing. She leant back and looked up through the leaves above her head. But then that was how they all were, surely, the people in the garden, they started out blindly on some path not too sure where it would lead them, but going forward all the same — what was it drove them on?

She and Bea, sharing that one bed for the first time, what was it had driven them on, to touch, to explore? Curiosity, of course, Eleanor smiled up at the leaves, but it was a little more than that, the kind of curiosity that carries with it the certainty of reward — like searching the parlour for the easter egg you know is there. And yet how tentative they had been! They had made this great leap and yet how little they had dared — it was daring enough, only the thought of it. To defy the natural order: that was how they would see it, down there in the garden. Walking in the sun, upholding the natural order.

She rose abruptly and walked back down the path to the formal gardens. All was much as it had been, children running between the rose beds, a few old men on the benches. She stood between the rows of benches looking down again at the scene. The cries of the children seemed to her louder and more piercing, the women carrying babies a little weary in the sun. What could she care that she and Bea had stood apart, unnatural? This was the natural world, she thought, in which she would have had to have her place, these tired people spending their brief summer Sundays in the park, among the staked roses.

* * * * * * * * * * * * * *

Eleanor closed the door and clicked down the latch. She untied the canvas blind at the top of the door and let it roll to the floor; the windows were already spread with newspaper for the night, and the shop swept. She hung her overall on the peg by the back entrance and turned to climb the stairs. At the top the cat curved against the banister, body rubbing along the grey-stained wall, mark of each evening's uneasy waiting for the shop's closing.

Eleanor sighed at the stain, 'You're marking the paint again,' and at the sound the cat bounded off down the passage and turned in at the kitchen entrance.

She carried her supper through to the front room. The accounts to do, no time tomorrow with her starting — what was to be done with her? Eleanor stared down at her plate — these tomatoes, no wonder they were selling slowly, quite tasteless. She would eat more of the spare vegetables, wouldn't she, that was the idea. Did she have a family? Came in regularly, didn't she, but no family, not children — not enough potatoes, Eleanor thought — but buying grapes for somebody. Of course she might have bought them for herself —you did that, she knew well enough, buying special things for yourself because no one else would, that could be it. There was probably a husband, though, his tastes a bit beyond their means by the look of her, going through her change. No children, so she didn't meet them in the usual places, then, standing around outside that school with their prams.

It was dangerous to think of having someone in the shop at all, not easy to get rid of. Thought you'd risk it — a little company, a little help with the lifting. All this for a little conversation. Here you are, as you always knew you would be, a lonely old woman. Eleanor put aside her plate and lit a cigarette. I don't believe that. Loneliness isn't the point — just another way of saying you are alone.

She had grown to appreciate that state, in which her mind was free from distractions. She was aware of what was passing in the world. To be alone was to be free to allow your faculties to range over things. She saw her surroundings as others could not whose senses were attuned to catch the feelings of those near them. She was free of the need to parry and anticipate the emanations of those standing close. Beyond the range of personal thrusts, the mechanisms seemed clearer to her. It was as if as Eleanor had walked the streets of towns, of London, of this village, the world had gradually been laid bare. She had worked in offices, silent behind her typewriter as others spoke of their dresses, their conquests, their failures. She had sat in cafes as families had spilled themselves onto her table, throwing their quarrels down among the sugar cube wrappings. She had visited old friends, and they had unburdened themselves to her. She saw them as if to the bone and said little.

Eleanor glanced at the violin case propped in the corner of the room — the orchestra was still there, of course, and those same friends. But empty, shallow — why seek them out? Loneliness was not important, better than the alternatives. Empty, like the letters those old friends sent. Wasted on her mother. She had needed no sympathy, anyway, then — it had been a long time and Eleanor had been glad to see her going away from that pain at last. All that was left of her, pain and a mangled body the doctors had torn at. Chasing disease through parts and organs of her like a desperate fox until it had run to earth, a final tumour near the heart. And her mother and the cancer she harboured had died gasping together.

Eleanor walked over to the window; the street below was quiet, the pavement empty but for the black bags huddled in shop doorways for the dust cart. Her mother had been fifty-five. A little over five years, she thought, before I start thinking it's going to get me. Her eyes swept the street for any sign of movement. As if she were expecting something, she had held herself apart, all these years. It was not that she minded, being alone. But was it to be this passing the time, always? The hope still there — that she wouldn't be wasted. She knew some things, after all. A flicker of movement caught her eye and she looked down: a thin dog came out of a doorway and trotted off down the street. Eleanor turned back to the table and the books spread out across it. She had this woman coming tomorrow. There was no help for it now, she was coming. She was much younger; she would talk too much, talk about her husband and whether to have a baby yet or to wait for his rise and if she saw herself as a mother. And she wanted to get to know the local women, she said. Better just have the baby and meet them in the nursery. Eleanor seized a pencil and bent over a column of figures; there was no need to keep her on, after all, she could be got rid of soon enough.

Later she straightened suddenly and laid down the pencil. It was still light, but the pub was open now and she could hear the juke-box playing.

She realised that she had forgotten to put her own rubbish out for the morning, and the back yard was full as it was. She turned on the shop lights and took the door off the latch. One by one she carried the bags through from the back and stacked them in the doorway, balanced so that the milkman would be able to reach the doorstep. She locked the door again and went out through the back yard; the usual smell of rotting vegetables lingered. Perhaps the girl could wash down the concrete.

Eleanor awoke early to sunlight falling across the foot of her bed. She went over to the window; a few clouds were gathering from the west, but there would be sun enough for a breakfast in the garden. She put the kettle on and set a tray with the larger teapot. It would be pleasant to linger over tea this morning. It was absurd that the sight of the sun shining of a morning should cheer her so, that she should be hurrying about aching to be out in it, not to miss a moment. She dressed anxiously, peering out of the window for clouds. The sun held, and Eleanor carried her tray out to the garden table, spread a blanket over the wet seat, and ate her cereal, smiling. Much later she sat with her hands cupped round a last, cooling mug of tea and watched a sparrow pecking her toast crumbs from the grass. It must be opening time. But the milk would be all right on the shop doorstep. She looked at her watch, and remembered the new woman, told to be there fifteen minutes ago.

She ran through: she was there, sitting on the doorstep next to the rubbish bags. Looking somehow small and defenceless, her arms round her knees.

Eleanor opened the door. 'I'm sorry — I was sitting in the garden, in the sunshine, and I quite forgot —'

The girl turned and jumped up. 'It's a beautiful day, isn't it?' Eleanor stood back to let her in. She was trying to be pleasant. For any length of time that would prove insufferable.

'Did you bring an overall, or anything? You'll get fairly dirty, otherwise.'

'These are old clothes, I don't think it matters if I get them dirty — unless you want me to wear something.'

'Present a uniform front to the customers, you mean? I don't think so.' Eleanor had taken her own overall off its peg. It looked limp and greyish and she didn't particularly want to put it on. She held it out by the neck and looked at it. Behind her Dee laughed suddenly and Eleanor jumped.

'Perhaps you could wear one of those butcher's aprons, blue and white canvas with pockets. I've always wanted to.'

'I don't see myself in a straw boater, thank you.' Eleanor shrugged her arms into the overall and looked at her watch. 'I'll be opening soon. I'm afraid your first job is one of the nastier ones. I'll show you,' and she led Dee to the back yard, 'this place smells — clean it, would you? There's a brush and broom and detergent just inside the back door.'

There was a lull at eleven and Eleanor put the kettle on in the kitchen upstairs. She came down again and out to the back door. She was out there on her hands and knees, scrubbing at the drain in the middle of the yard. The air smelt antiseptic. She had thrown her pullover over the water tap and was in her shirt sleeves. She looked a rather fat waif, and earnest. Harmless.

'Have you nearly finished?' Eleanor called, 'I've put the kettle on — tea all right?'

Dee sat back on her heels, 'I'd like some tea — I think it's all done here now.'

Eleanor brought the smaller teapot down from the shelf. She stared uncertainly at the biscuits — she looked as if she ate biscuits, and she must be tired after the dustbins all morning. Eleanor added the biscuits and took the tray down into the shop. There was a customer in, wanting oranges: Dee had tried to put them all into one bag and split it, was dividing them into two new ones. Eleanor watched the customer out of the shop.

'You don't really need to put oranges in bags. Most of the women have their shopping bags with them, they can go straight in. If someone hasn't got one, you can only fit four of the smaller ones in a paper bag. I'd better show you how to close them, hadn't I, I thought you were going to break those two as well.'

Dee had managed to get the till open and put the money away. 'I thought I knew — I've watched women do it, after all — but I think I lost heart in mid-twist, or something.' She leant against the till, 'And I'm afraid I don't know how to use your scales, either.'

'I'll show you, it's not difficult. But we should have tea first — there's another chair in the back somewhere.' It was unnerving. Eleanor felt as if she might be mangling this woman's feelings. Like blighting a child's world carelessly, and without knowing it. Perhaps she had ceased to be able to get on with someone, someone less withdrawn. She didn't want to per-

35

secute her.

'My name's Eleanor. What shall I call you?'

Dee blushed and bent her head over her mug, 'My name's Daisy. I'm called Dee, which goes a bit to the other extreme – of austerity, I mean – but I prefer it for want of anything else.'

Eleanor noticed Dee's eyes lighting on the biscuit packet, and she pushed it over. 'You must be hungry after all that scrubbing.'

Dee nodded, and took two biscuits from the packet. She broke them into sections and packed the pieces methodically into her mouth. The wadding served as a protection against the silence that was falling over their tea-break. Dee felt physically uncomfortable; muscles twitched painfully all over her body, her head throbbed. She sat tensed in her chair; her body had taken upon itself the expression of her discomfort at intruding so visibly upon this other woman. It was as if Eleanor had no public space around her where strangers could approach without danger. It was none of it neutral but all angry, spiked, with barriers and defences and obstacles. Dee felt almost sore, as if her skin had been pricked by needles. She hung over her mug. Her mind was paralysed with the rest: was she like this all the time, was there something that was making her suspicious, was she retreating so far because she thought Dee might somehow be after her? Dee looked at her watch – it was more than half over. In a couple of hours she could get away; she needed to know what she was meeting – she had been unprepared. She felt disoriented, as at sea as if she were meeting herself: herself at work, perhaps, someone as wary of the world. And she didn't seem to have the means to deal with her own mechanisms, if that's what they were, in this woman. She seemed uncontrolled, free in some way from expected restraints, frightening.

Eleanor watched Dee chewing her way through her biscuits; she looked altogether like a hamster, curled in her chair. Vaguely rodent-coloured – the brown trousers, the reddish-brown shirt, both baggy and shapeless, and that odd hair, that was straight but stuck out slightly from the crown of her head like some species of dog. Her eyes over the mug had a slightly glassy look, Eleanor noticed, that added to the hamster effect, as if her mind was slightly away from her body and had ceased to animate the space behind her eyes. Eleanor held herself still, watching; Dee stared inward. What was she thinking, Eleanor wondered? She put a hand across the space between them and lifted the tea-pot. Dee's eyes flickered and refocused.

36

'I'll put the tray upstairs and then I'll show you the things in the shop, shall I?'

'Same time tomorrow, then.'

Dee stepped backwards out of the doorway and ran down the main street, letting herself run as fast as she could, swerving round shoppers and prams and dogs as if she were carefree, a young boy, and the running a release enough in itself. She stuttered to a stop in the lane, dizzy already, her legs weak. She walked carefully the rest of the way back to the house.

There was some soup on the stove; she lit a burner under it and walked to the bottom of the stairs. 'Ann?' She wanted Ann to be in, she didn't want to have to hold her thoughts back, make them shorter or more finished. She wanted to be able to think aloud before the details of the morning hardened — like drying concrete, there was only a short time that she could use to make patterns, to experiment, to make sense. And Ann had gone off somewhere. Dee went back to the kitchen. There were no bowls in the cupboard. She crossed to the sink, and saw Ann through the window bent over the vegetable patch.

'What are you doing? I'm not ruining some plan by eating this soup, am I?'

Ann straightened up and picked her way back to the path from the turned earth. 'No, I made it for lunch — good, isn't it. I'm hoeing the lettuces. Mr MacGregor in Beatrix Potter was always hoeing lettuces. I can't quite believe I'm doing it right — but it looks authentic enough, doesn't it, the row of bright green lettuces and a little heap of withering weeds.' She paused, looking back at the neat earth. 'Of course, the sheep and the goats. No wonder it felt odd — I've been sitting in judgement on the vegetables and upholding the patriarchal order.' Ann glanced over at Dee standing on the path, spooning soup into her mouth. 'You look tired — was it hard, after all?'

'It was an ordeal, I'm exhausted from it.' Dee sank down onto the grass, 'She'd forgotten I was coming, and I had to sit on the step. I don't think she wanted me to be there at all.' Ann had gone back to the lettuces, and the scrape of the hoe sounded in the silence. 'But it was more personal than that — it was as though I were a threat to her privacy in a very immediate way, like an unwanted guest — I felt as if I were in her bedroom, almost, rather than her fruit shop.'

Dee lay back in the grass, 'I felt too large all the time.'

Ann laughed; she could see Dee looming over the vegetables. 'But the woman who runs that place isn't so small, is she? I hadn't noticed her as tiny and neat and precise and with minute feet or anything, such as might make you feel gargantuan.'

Dee leaned up on one elbow and picked a sharp pebble from the grass. Gargantuan, she thought, as if there's some substance to it. She hurled the stone at Ann's shin. It missed, and she picked up a handful and began to throw them: 'I am not gargantuan. Your mind is full of shit about beautiful body types.' The stones had begun to hit and Ann retreated across the garden. 'Your body beautiful stereotypes oppress me —'

'I didn't say you were gargantuan', Ann protested, out of range, 'you said you felt large, and I was embroidering, that's all. I like picturesque words.' Dee was being unreasonable in that particular way that meant that she couldn't deal with a free flow of words. Ann looked at the lettuces. She would enjoy hoeing the lettuces and she would not let this curb irritate her. She picked up the hoe again: 'Go on,' she said.

Dee flung the rest of the stones down. 'I'm not explaining it right at all. She isn't small, she's rather tall, and thin. She wears brown and her face is sallow. She has what I think are called mobile features — that was part of the trouble, that I kept catching traces of sneers and she would make an effort to smile, and grimace instead.' Dee plucked at the grass; she had not described the scene, had not got what she wanted out if it. 'She was almost rude to me — very abrupt, and then she would seem to regret it and try and say something soothing. She didn't seem able to come up with ordinary politenesses.'

'She sounds rather like you — like you behave when you're somewhere you'd rather not be, or don't approve of, or something.' Ann looked at Dee curiously: 'Are you sure that wasn't all it was — you tend to do that with people you don't know, before you decide they're acceptable. You haven't had to face the weight of your own silences.' Ann left the hoe on the ground and sat next to Dee on the path, reaching in Dee's shirt pocket for cigarettes. She lit two and passed one across. 'If you were both doing that to each other, no wonder you're exhausted. You've probably finished her, too, poor woman.'

'I did make a few friendly overtures,' Dee said; but she felt relieved. If it were only that. 'D'you think I'm as bad as that? I felt as if she was full of hate and contempt for me.'

'She's probably had years of extra practice at putting people off. She'll get used to you, and be stuffing soggy apples into your hands before you know it.'

Dee laughed and leaned into Ann's arm: 'You're much too reassuring – you should be thinking of the risks. She might knife me tomorrow morning, for all you know.'

'That's an unwholesome stereotype too, the deranged spinster – is she a spinster?'

'I don't know for sure, but it's her shop, so I suppose so. She wasn't very forthcoming about personal details, dear. I can tell you her name's Eleanor. And she doesn't wear make-up.'

'That doesn't mean anything.'

'It does here. Haven't you noticed, in the bus queue in the morning, all those women going in to work, and the pensioners with their passes, even? There's a line of old withered faces wrapped in headscarves, and the wind blowing into them. And they all have bright lipstick on, or blue eye-shadow. It's horrible, makes them look quite hideous and desperate. Of course, the women at work used to wear it, I didn't find that surprising. I knew they had to keep up some appearance or other. Or they were younger and expected something to come of it.'

Dee's voice trailed off. No nearer to understanding – why did they not see they didn't have to go on with it? Perhaps there was no escaping the pressures, it was all one, inescapable. Couldn't they nibble at the edges, did it all have to be as taboo as walking naked down the street? Did Eleanor not wear it, then, because she saw it as a capitulation? Her clothes, her manner, was she trying to put herself outside, to refuse to make concessions? Of course not. What was this power and freedom she was endowing Eleanor with? She might perhaps have managed to withdraw from a few necessities, have given up a few appearances. All the worse then – she probably saw it as a defeat. Failing as a woman. And could get only resentment from the unfairness of that.

But Dee was not sure. She remembered Eleanor standing at the till, working out prices in her head – abstracted, her hands stuffed into her overall pockets. Poised, concentrated; surely she was too complete, with a sense of her own completeness, to be bounded by – what people thought. But there was nothing else. How useful the idea of individual freedom was when you wanted to believe that someone might have escaped some form of oppression or other. Dee ground out her cigarette in the grass; it was foolish to expect so much. It was no use anyway, even if it might make her time at the shop more pleasant — there was no future in this one woman's managing to achieve some kind of independence. Eleanor might believe in individual freedom, but she did not.

'They have to go on with it, I suppose,' she said.

'Well, what would they be saying if they didn't? People have to have something to put in its place.'

'Yes,' said Dee, 'I gave it up because I was trying to be a hippie and be flowing and cool. I used to wear purple and embroider 'daisy' in full on my shirts and wear my hair as long as it would go.' She looked up, smiling — and Ann was on her feet suddenly, turning towards the house.

'I can see an idea, it's very vivid, I don't want to lose it.' Ann had run off round the corner.

Dee picked up the hoe that lay by the side of the path and stood looking down at the lettuces. She could not hoe them, she thought, they would leave so much room for her thoughts to go back to old times, those old choices she'd once made so lightly for no reason that now had worth. She turned and walked back to the house, the hoe bumping along the ground behind her.

* * * * * * * * * * * * * * *

Ann walked slowly along the pavement. Did she look old enough? There only seemed to be police cars about in the streets. She would say she was coming home from a party. She looked at her watch: it was half-past twelve, they couldn't stop her walking the streets at half-past twelve. She turned off the main road onto a quiet tree-lined street, the trees now white and yellow with blossom in the lamp light. She stopped under a tree and stared up through its laden branches to the filtered yellow light; it was beautiful, the layers of petals, their clear outlines shifting in a faint breeze. But it was cold: she should have put a sweater on. Her hand reached into the top pocket of her army jacket – she had the cigarettes. Another side road, she was getting near. If Miss Hubert were there, what would she do? If she weren't? I can wait, thought Ann, and she will meet me in the road. Perhaps she will invite me in – surely if she sees me she will invite me in.

'What are you doing here, Ann, at this time of night?'

'I don't know, Miss Hubert.'

'Well, you'd better come in out of the cold for some tea. And then you must go home.'

Perhaps she would drive her home in her car, and she would sit over her tea and store up the inside of Miss Hubert's flat, find her christian name on an envelope.

Ann thrust her hands into her jacket pockets and walked faster, the fear of losing sudden and violent as she turned into Miss Hubert's road – she could even now be missing her, parking her car, walking round it to the front door, her key ready for the latch. Ann could see the door now – the car was there, she was home already. She should have come earlier, it was hopeless to have come this evening, she should have waited for a time they went to bed early, why had they stayed up so late when she was ready – was there a light on, still? Ann moved quietly up the road, keeping close to the hedge. There was a light in an upper window. She crossed the street to the lamp post opposite her door, she would look out of the window and see her before she went to bed. She would come down in her dressing-gown, tousled perhaps and concerned. She was concerned for her pupil's well-being, she would ask searching questions, Ann thought, and I shall be able to confess, I am in love with you. And she will console me and I shall visit her.

Ann settled her back against the lamp post and lit a cigarette. The kind she smoked. The scrape of the match was loud in the quiet street and Ann stared at the window — surely she had heard, she would look out now? The curtain did not move. Ann leaned her head on the ridged post and half-closed her eyes. When she knows that I love her she will tell me her name. I will not tell anyone what it is, I will not allude to her friendship in school, I will be discreet. But it is awful to have nothing, does she know how I feel when she bends over my picture, sometimes her hand is on the back of my chair and I want to lean back against it, I want her to know what I am feeling. She must look out and see me. Ann flung her cigarette into the roadway; the glowing end made an arc through the air and landed still alight. Ann stepped into the road and trod heavily on the butt, her plimsoll squeaking on the tarmac — but the curtain did not move. She lit another cigarette and leaned again; the light had gone out in the window. Now she would look out before getting into bed. Ann flicked ash toward the gutter. She cannot be asleep yet. I could ring the doorbell, she would let me in. I could say I was very miserable about my exams, I'm her best pupil, she'd have to let me in. And artists are always neurotic and unstable, she'd be worried about me. Ann shifted and crammed her cold hands into her armpits. She didn't want to be so pathetic, Miss Hubert should see that she was above that, being juvenile, could be discreet. She was serious and odd; Miss Hubert would know that when she looked out.

It was cold and her shoulders ached. There was some loose gravel in the gutter. Ann picked up a handful of stones and threw them across the road. A few bounced on the pavement and the rest rattled on the bonnet of her car. Ann waited, but no movement showed at the window. She turned and walked back down the street. If only her mother hadn't heard her go out. If only she hadn't come down and found the back window open she would be all right.

* * * * * * * * * * * * * *

42

The smooth round wood was cool against her arm. Ann carried it against her hip as women carried their babies. Her best piece, her favourite that she had spent all spring over, so no wonder, she thought, that she carried it like an infant, her hand cupped over the swell of its legs.

She turned down the street, the pavement dusty, the leaves on the trees heavy and dark with dirt and the age of July. But the clouds were thick enough for rain: she would be at home, making tea, staring at the weather, waiting for the end of term. Ann turned another corner; why was she doing this, she asked herself, wasn't all that, the past, best left alone? But she wanted to manage life so that things were not always being left, messes she had made and could only hurry away from, hoping to forget, to start again. Ann noticed a bench, someone had installed it overlooking the churchyard. She sat down and put the wooden figure on the bench beside her, her hand caressing its head for a moment. She was only twenty and already there were so many people she had left behind, could no longer speak to. They were the ones she most wanted to go on speaking to, or else why should she have loved them? And now that those feelings could be acknowledged, given their proper significance, she could go back and reclaim the past.

How many times now had she said in meetings, I was in love with my art teacher; each time she felt more pleasure in the memory of it — it seemed like the most encompassing experience of her life. Gradually she had been able to take it up, it was not a phase, something she might perhaps get through and must meanwhile play down, it was the first of her loves. So Amy must be told, it wasn't something she wanted to go on hiding as if she were still ashamed of it. Ann smiled at her wooden statue and lifted it into her lap; there were other things, of course, there was Amy's quick grin and the way she had of flicking her hair back with a twitch of her head, there was the way she stood intent over some piece, a picture — her hands gesticulating, making it all clear to you. Ann smiled: she had not forgotten. She picked up the sculpture and walked down the street, turned a last corner and rang Amy Hubert's doorbell. She heard her coming down the stairs.

'Ann! Hello,' Amy swung the door wider, 'what can I do for you?'

'I've brought some work I'd like to show you, if that's all right.'

'Of course, come in — I'm on the upper floor.'

She led the way upstairs, 'Come into the kitchen, I was going to make some tea — how have you been getting on?'

'Oh — fine.'

Ann drew the sculpture from behind her back and set it on the table. She sat on a stool and watched Amy filling the kettle; she would talk to her through her statue, her beautiful dark wood woman.

Amy set the kettle on the gas and turned round, 'Goodness, is that it? I didn't know you were working with wood.'

'I don't often, it seemed right for her, though. It's yew — very hard.'

Amy moved over to the table and picked it up: 'It's not poisonous, like the berries, is it?' She laughed and carried it a little way towards the window. It was lumpy, thick limbs reaching from a roughly-carved torso. Only the head, thrown back, had been polished smooth. Not quite fertile, a little more self-conscious than that, Amy thought. Look at those knees, flung apart. She noticed then that one breast — they were irregularly shaped, dissimilar — had been carefully polished. She placed it on the window sill for a moment. There was power in it, it sat well, casually. But what was Ann trying to say? Amy carried it back to the table, her fingers feeling the polished head. There was Ann, sitting so thin and small, sitting so curled up on her stool; it was the woman that Ann would never be, Amy thought, so thick and lush and spread out.

'It's beautiful,' she said, 'powerful, and sweeping, and it sits well, doesn't it.'

Ann nodded, 'Yes, she's powerful.'

'A relaxed, giving presence. The contemporary ideal — you do make it seem worth trying for.' Amy smiled at the little wooden figure.

'She's not, she's not the contemporary ideal.' Ann uncurled herself abruptly and leaned her hands on the table: 'She's not giving at all. She's self-contained, she knows what she wants —'

'But powerful women, full of power like that, sexual energy,' she was not a child after all, Amy thought, she could say such things, 'must give out what they have to the world, it's what they need to do, what the world needs from them.'

Didn't Ann have other teachers now, that she could argue with? There ought to be people at that art college that she could get her theories of life from, there was no need for her to come back — there were already so many pupils battening on her, feeding on her – she had to buoy them up, place them here and there, she really hadn't time to take on Ann, to take up an old burden. It was an adolescent carving, so naked and arrogant. Amy stuffed teabags into the pot; it was not so easy to be the woman you wanted. She thought of the easel next door. She should not have started on Greg's portrait, she kept finding herself wanting to paint someone else, a kind of symbol-Greg with big hands and a bowler hat and wearing Greg's rugger shorts. She couldn't do that of course, it had to be a portrait of a young man, a lithe young man with charm and wit, a sensual young man. She had him lounging in a deckchair; he was capable of such controlled relaxation, there was a sense always when she looked at him of muscles under the surface. There was something of that about Ann's figure, she realised, perhaps they both were in awe of the physical, felt themselves not part of it.

Amy put the mugs on the table: 'I'm not sure that it's realistic, Ann, that's all – but I envy her.'

Ann looked up from her hands on the table, she smiled: 'So do I.'

But she looked hurt, Amy saw the droop of her mouth, she needed more. 'Would you like to see what I'm working on? It's in the other room.'

Ann stared at the easel, the lightly blocked-in figure: 'What a menacing posture.' The man lounged, his feet carelessly apart, his head on one side staring out at her, the pose of a predator nonchalant of its prey.

'It's wonderful,' Ann said simply.

'It's a picture of my fiance.'

Ann gulped down some tea and scalded herself; there were tears in her eyes. Amy had moved so suddenly away from her, suddenly there was nothing she could do to touch her – that was clear, she could do nothing about this. She was helpless in the face of Amy's decision – what had made her do it, she knew nothing about Amy's life, would never know – could only feel betrayed by it. It came out from nowhere and cut off the Amy she had loved in the past; marriage sealed off her experience, it would be something she could not go back to any more. An irrevocable end.

'Are you sure you want to marry him? I'm sorry –' Ann gestured at the easel, 'it's that picture – you make him so frightening.'

Amy sighed, 'I know, it comes over like that, doesn't it – I was thinking perhaps it's fear of physicality – he's so sure and controlled – I was thinking that there was that in your piece too.'

Amy flicked the hair out of her eyes; Ann saw the gesture and turned away — there was nothing she could do. The world went on inexorable, women married if they could and only the odd and the frightened ended up different. All those psychology text-books that explained homosexuality as a failure to come to terms with one's fear of the opposite sex. Perhaps they were right after all. Ann stared down at Amy's bed in the corner, a striped bedspread thrown over it; she was helpless at the weight of everything bearing her down.

'My woman's meant to be different,' she said bleakly, 'it's not meant to be a threatening sort of power.'

Amy brooded over Greg; she'd started the picture to show him somehow that there was use in her art — he seemed to overlook it rather — so painting him was a way of bringing the two things together. But he did look menacing, it was true — how could she show him that as a link between her involvement in him and in painting?

'I suppose women think of men in general as frightening — and of course they have privileges —' Amy turned her back on the easel, 'but we can't leave them alone for all that, can we? We have to get on with making things better together.' She glanced at Ann, why was she so hunched, there at the end of the room? 'Would you like some more tea? I'm still thirsty.' Ann nodded and Amy took the mugs through to the kitchen.

'Marriage isn't going to help things,' Ann muttered. Did she always have to shuffle off into a corner while other women, the ones with husbands, changed the things that mattered?

'Don't you approve of marriage, then?'

Ann shrugged, leaning in the doorway: 'No, I don't, I suppose. But it's more than that.' She moved over to the kitchen window and looked out over the patch of lawn underneath. 'I suppose I resent the whole system.'

'There's no getting away from it, though,' Amy sat at the table, her hands around her mug; the statue was still there, she reached out her hand to it, 'married or not, men are an important part of my life.'

Ann stood at the window; it was hopeless, she should leave now, there was no life in the things she had come to say.

'I came to give you the statue, I made it for you.'

Ann felt the accusation rising into her voice. Why should she keep silent, just so that Amy could be spared?

'I came to tell you that I was in love with you at school.' She turned to face the room, 'And I don't think things should be secret. I'm not ashamed of it. It was very important to me.'

Amy drew her hand away from the statue. It was absurd to be frightened, there were plenty of them like that, they soon got over it.

'I think that happens to a lot of girls.'

Ann walked over to the table and picked up her mug: 'I expect it does.' But she could not stand by the table, standing there she felt — she was made somehow to feel — unreasonable. She went back to the window — she only wanted to explain: 'And most of them are forced to think of it as unimportant, not the real thing. I am a lesbian, Amy, and I loved you.'

She drank her tea. The silence lengthened between them, Ann staring out of the window; it was over. It had been pointless, but it was over. She only wanted to leave. The table lay between her and the door — would Amy try to stop her? But it was over. She turned and walked to the door, keeping her body gathered in close, skirting chairs, keeping her eyes off the statue. Her voice came clipped: 'The source of inspiration should have the product. As a wedding present.' She had reached the kitchen door, the front door, was running down the stairs. In the street she looked across at the lamp post opposite. There is a time to give up on reactivating the past, she thought, there must be an end to it.

In the kitchen Amy sat inert, hearing the doors of her flat shut one by one. She could not move, had nothing to say. She did not know how to push Ann's intrusive declaration far enough away. She held her hands clasped in her lap; had she done something to encourage it, surely there was nothing in her that had brought it on? My silence has driven her away, she thought, looking round the empty room, but what did she expect from me?

The statue sat casually on the table. That is not me, I can't have it, thought Amy suddenly. She picked it up and ran out, down the stairs and into the road. I thought homosexuals fell in love with each other, she thought, running down the street, the statue clutched to her chest, what does Ann want from me? She stopped at the corner — there was a small figure wandering down the pavement, one hand idly brushing the hedges.

'Ann!' she shouted, 'Ann, come back!'

Ann stopped short. After a moment she turned around. She stood still but Amy did not move towards her. 'It's hopeless,' she muttered to herself, 'what are you going back for again?' She walked reluctantly up the road.

Amy held the statue in her arms and looked at the pavement, the hedges. She must not smile, she must not look — Ann must not think she was calling her back for — it wasn't a reunion, did Ann know that? When she was still too far away she held out the statue.

'You must have this. It's not me.'

Ann stopped, her hands in her pockets.

'I don't want it.'

Amy came a step closer, she must give it.

'Yes you do,' she said, and knew that it was true. And suddenly she pitied Ann standing hunched in the road, 'It's beautiful, Ann, but it's more about what you want than what I do.'

She thrust the thing at Ann, at her chest; Ann's hands came out of her pockets to meet it — the statue hung between them.

'It's more about what you can get, Ann. I'm going to marry Greg, remember?'

She took a pace back, letting her hands fall, flicking her hair away.

'He wouldn't appreciate her at all.'

* * * * * * * * * * * * * * *

'I try to understand you, Nellie.' Mrs Hardy leaned back in her armchair. Her head moved restlessly from side to side; the pain in her back perhaps, or the hopelessness of her daughter's silence.

'I know that, mother.'

Across the fireplace Eleanor sighed and put down her tea-cup. The room smelt acrid, of cheap coal.

'You're thirty-five now, and not getting any younger.'

Eleanor smiled faintly: 'I know that too, mother.'

Mrs Hardy closed her eyes. She was very tired, too tired almost to go on.

'Won't you tell me something, dear, something about it all?'

Eleanor stared into the fire; it was not that she wanted so much to hold back from her mother, she would not so much mind trying to explain to her. She should understand, after all, the attempt to reduce your needs to the minimum, to make as few demands as possible of the world. Less chance then of refusal. And there was a certain dry purity to be had from it all, a satisfaction in not spreading yourself more than necessary. She should understand that, after having to ask for more than she got for so long.

Her, coming out of the offices, dragging Eleanor by the hand — must have been quite small then, having to change schools for some reason — and they'd been there hours, begging money for a uniform, had come away at last with not half enough. 'Which half d'you want dressed, then,' she'd said to him, 'the top or the bottom?' Turning on the steps, white: 'I'm damned if we'll go in there again.' Of course they always had to, to go somewhere.

Wanted her daughter to be able to take all she wanted, be free to ask and get it all. Lavishly, not dress-making and a widow's pension. And that meant marriage, thought Eleanor wearily, that was the way out, out of the office. She was only a typist, wasn't she, and what future was there in that?

'I don't want to put myself in someone's hands, ma,' Eleanor gestured vaguely, 'can't you see that I'd never feel safe? I must look after myself, that's what I care about. What security is, for me.'

'But it's such a hard life.'

Mrs Hardy's head twisted as the pain ground into her back, she could not at once control the movement, the shock in her face as it came at her.

Eleanor looked up from the fire, 'Won't you go to the doctor with that pain, for god's sake?'

'Damn doctors. Give me another cup of tea.'

Eleanor filled the cups again. As Mrs Hardy drank Eleanor crouched at the fire-place building up the fire, methodically placing coals one by one as if she were laying the foundations of a wall. 'I'm saving my money,' she said slowly, frowning over her task, 'there'll soon be enough for me to buy a lease on a business, I think —'

'But Nellie, don't you want to marry?'

Eleanor kept her eyes on the fire; she would go on, she thought, why should her mother not want to hear how she intended to live, preferred to? 'I think,' she said, 'I think perhaps that you think of marriage as something rather better than it usually is, ma — he died so quickly, and then you remembered the best bits. And of course people tell you it's desirable, but then that's because they're stuck with it, maybe. And your husband can go off any time — it used to happen all the time here — if he wasn't dead he was bored —'

Mrs Hardy trembled with anger: 'How can you talk such nonsense, Nellie? I never said marriage was bliss, did I? It's security, that's all, and a little comfort in your old age if you're lucky. How can you look at me and say such things?' She set her cup down with a rattle. 'I could never get a decent job all the years before the war, and when that was over I was out again, and where'd I be now, if it weren't for your money keeping me alive?'

Eleanor stood up, 'Well, it does that all right, doesn't it? What d'you want to be someone's mother-in-law for? I'm going to fill the coal scuttle.'

'Well, you've built the fire so's it'll burn all night.'

Eleanor turned at the door and grinned: 'I'll keep you up, then, arguing.'

'You won't — I'm a sick old woman.' Mrs Hardy waved her on: 'Don't hang there with the door open, lord! Fill the scuttle if you must, but get on with it!'

When Eleanor came back with the coal her mother had sunk into her chair. For a moment Eleanor stared down at her before Mrs Hardy's eyes started open, 'That took you long enough.'

Eleanor nodded at the door, 'I've put the old bucket outside the door as well, saves you going out to the shed for a bit.'

The eyes flickered off her face, fixed on the wall over the mantel: 'So you're not getting married, then.'

'I don't think so, not really — ma, I've been thinking —'

'You'll regret it, you know.'

'I've been thinking about —'

Mrs Hardy shook her head, 'No one'll thank you for it, you can be sure of that.'

'No one thanks me for living as it is, ma.' Eleanor spoke flatly. She shook her head irritably, as if to clear some fog lying between the two of them, 'What are you getting at?'

'It's something about London, isn't it? You've not been the same since you went down there, too much alone down there, I'd say.' Mrs Hardy still contemplated the wall. It remained solid, the same wall; but it was the wall that she always watched, tracing the swirls in the wallpaper, trying to order things into the pattern on the wall. Once it had been the bills — that big swirl over the clock the rent, that came first, and the little ones coming off it, some weeks she would have money to fill those out, the grocer, the coal. Then further up it swelled out again, once she had used one of those up there, the one on the left, she'd made a wedding dress and that swirl had been an outing to the sea. She remembered it, finding the pattern again in the wall. Now, though, it was the ache that banged and hummed in her back; she put it on the wall and it throbbed round the swirls, drew in round the fiddly bits and rushed out again in the swelling rounds. Mrs Hardy would watch it from a distance, grateful for the little space between her and the wall, for the regularity of the pattern. She knew the rhythm of it and it could hardly hurt her; she had only to keep it there, swirling round and round on the wall.

She drew her eyes back to her daughter — brown, she was wearing brown again, surely that skirt was longer than they were wearing them, these days? And she didn't want to get married. That was what the girls always used to say, but that was right after the war, twenty years ago, Nellie and her friends, a long time ago now. Perhaps there was a time to stop worrying about all that, Mrs Hardy thought, looking across at Eleanor hunched up in her chair, frowning — she hadn't really time to think about all that, any more.

'So you're not getting married,' she said.

Eleanor looked across at her: she was resigned to it now, all of a sudden; why was that Eleanor wondered, what could she have come upon all at once — was it that she had looked over and seen her unmarriageable, seen her as a spinster? Eleanor followed the line of brass buttons on her skirt, did she look past it, so that even her own mother had to give her up, a lost cause? It made no difference that she wasn't quite fighting that battle, she thought, though of course it ought, she should be above such things. Her handbag was under the chair — she reached down for it and fished out a packet of Players.

'Still smoking them — men's cigarettes.'

'D'you want one?' Eleanor flicked the packet open.

Her mother grunted: 'Ech, why not, what's the harm?' She leant forward for the light and settled back into her chair, stretching out her feet. She expanded a little, smiled; there was something to be had from these small pleasures that came to you unexpectedly, nothing you'd anticipated, nothing very special, but a little extra all the same. Under the gentle haze of the tobacco smoke her mind could range a little farther: 'You want to buy a business, did you say, dear? Do you know how to run one, do you think?'

'I've read books about it — it's a shop I mean. A stores, or something.' Eleanor paused, 'Ma, I've been thinking that I could get a shop, just rent it perhaps, and we could both live in it.' Her mother made no sound; she hurried on, 'You wouldn't have to do anything in it, of course, but I'd be there to look after you — carry the coal and such. We could look for one round here if you like, near your friends — they could come and visit you — what do you think?'

Mrs Hardy held the cigarette tightly between her fingers; it had betrayed her — that moment of pleasure — and now Nellie wanted to take everything away from her, send her off somewhere.

'I'm quite happy here, Nellie,' she said. Perhaps Nellie was only thinking that she was lonely — but she no longer felt alone. How could she live with Nellie always there, after all this time, Nellie always watching? If she would just settle herself properly so that she could stop worrying, that was all Nellie need do.

'Why don't you find a shop, it might be just the thing for you, dear.' She dropped her cigarette vaguely into her saucer, and nodded her head, 'It sounds quite a good idea, yes, but you don't want me cluttering the place up, I'm much better here.'

'But if you're not well, mother, if you can't lift things —'

'Oh, Mrs Hughes sends her boy round to bring the coal in, so I'm all right there, quite all right.' Mrs Hardy nodded desperately, up and down: 'I'm quite all right, really.'

But perhaps Nellie couldn't have her shop if she was helping her with the rent here, was that it? Her eyes sought the wall, but the pattern jumped; she would have to leave — the knowledge tore across the wall, dizzily rolling and snapping, careering out of control.

'I don't want to move.' It had slipped out —she had not meant to say it, of course Nellie wanted her shop. But couldn't she have waited, just a little longer? 'I'm an old woman.'

'You're not fifty-five, ma —'

'I feel old, Nellie, too old to move.'

Mrs Hardy shut her lips tight. She mustn't say any more, go weedling and pleading to her daughter. She must do as she wanted, it was her money, and she would bear it. She sat back in her chair and set her teeth. Eleanor stared at her mother sitting rigid, stock still, opposite her. For a long time she watched the unmoving features, the hands gripping the arms of the chair. Her mother would not meet her gaze. At last Eleanor shook herself slightly and took out another cigarette. She jammed it between her teeth and spoke indistinctly, fumbling for a match.

'Well, if you don't like the idea then we shan't do it, of course. I thought it might appeal to you, that's all.'

She stopped, her mother had not moved, it was clear that she was not listening; Eleanor reached over and covered her mother's hand: 'Ma, I'm not going to force you to move if you don't want to! For god's sake, you must stay here as long as you want!' She was almost shouting. Mrs Hardy turned her head slowly and they looked at each other in silence.

* * * * * * * * * * * * * * *

It was early, the shop was just open, but already the whole-saler's lorry had been and gone. Dee leant in the doorway, her arms shaking from the sacks and crates she had carried inside. Eleanor shut the till and came out to her.

'Let's have a smoke out here before we put that stuff away.' She upended an empty crate and sat down.

Dee let her legs fold under her and landed on the doorstep, 'Did you do all that lifting by yourself, before? I'm exhausted from it.'

Eleanor looked down: 'I did it by myself all right,' she laughed, 'but much more slowly.'

Dee felt in her pockets, 'Damn, I've forgotten my fags — is the news-agent open yet, d'you know?'

'Here,' Eleanor pushed a packet at her, 'have one of mine.' She watched while Dee lit a cigarette. It was surprising how quickly she'd grown used to having Dee about the place, she thought, it was almost as if she blended in well with the surroundings. At one with the fruit and vegetables? Not quite that. Dee sat curled on the step. Was it that she took up so little space, somehow? Eleanor smiled — there was that hamster look again, partly that was what she meant, that air of intense concentration, concentration turned on whatever it might be, her cigarette, the scales, a crate to be lifted. She seemed to give things her attention and yet to be able to keep back what she found. I ought to find that disconcerting, Eleanor thought, in a way it is what I do myself. But she seems to find what she sees less of a burden. Perhaps she sees less, and that is all. Or perhaps she finds something in it all that I've missed. She puzzles me, she thought, she is too wary, says nothing of herself. A new specimen, not one I've come across before. Worth investigating, it might be.

She picked up her crate and carried it inside as a customer hesitated on the step. 'We are open, if you're wanting something,' she called, 'just getting the deliveries sorted out.'

'Oh well then, I'll come in now.'

She came, the first of a stream. Eleanor weighed plums and apples and broad beans. Dee stored the new provisions around the shop and served more customers, rattling new potatoes into the bottom of shopping baskets, putting ripe peaches in bags, practising the flick of the wrist that closed the bag without bruising the fruit. Women came in ceaselessly, hurriedly, as though the promise in the faint morning sky of a hot summer's day had thrown them out of bed scheming, organising, planning a picnic perhaps, a supper in the garden. They bought special fruit shyly, packing plums into their baskets with secret smiles, they bought lettuces, lavished extra money on cucumbers. Eleanor and Dee were caught up in the rush, whirling round the shop faster and faster; it was easy, absorbing, gratifying to satisfy their customers' needs, their luxurious whims.

By eleven o'clock the shop had emptied. The women were home in their kitchens, frowning over their salad bowls; in their gardens, testing the luxury of a peach eaten on the patio in bare feet. On the road home they gave their children plums that fell in the dust and rolled. Dee counted coppers into the till as the shop steadied and fell silent. Eleanor came down the stairs carrying the tea tray: the women's mood had affected her, she felt an urgency, a seeking; it was a day for fantasy and experiment.

She turned her eye on Dee, waiting at the till for her tea: 'Do you live by yourself down here?'

Dee thought of Ann, of the flowers she would pick on the way home, for once. Of that old hammock, they could mend it this afternoon and hang it for the evening. She smiled, taking her mug from the tray: 'No, I live with another woman in a house we've rented just outside the village.'

Eleanor stopped, her hand arrested over the sugar bowl. Lord, so that was it. Her hand trembled, and she drew it back — so that was what she was investigating. It went on did it — of course it did. What was odd about it, though? That they still came out to the country to live by themselves, that was odd — she thought they lived in London, in the cities, out in the open, went about declaring themselves. The young ones, at any rate. 'How old are you?' she asked.

Dee's eyes flickered, she was not really attending to the conversation, was thinking of the sun, the quiet garden, how she would get Ann into the garden for a talk — had she missed something, what was going on? She peered across at Eleanor, she wasn't jumping to conclusions, was she. 'I'm twenty-nine,' she said lightly, puzzled.

'I see,' said Eleanor.

She saw that of course, but there was much that she did not see — what was it like for them, here, why had they left the city — they must have been there, where else did you find them, she thought — what were they like together, was it possible? Was it any more possible?

Ann had carried a table out into the sun. In the afternoon Dee sat reading her book while Ann stared at a sketch.

'You're not drawing me, are you?' Dee said, looking up to find Ann squinting at her.

'Not as you are now, this is of you, but I started it before — I've nearly finished it. You can see it in a minute.'

Dee laid down her book and stretched: 'You know, I think Eleanor has realised I'm a lesbian.'

'How's that?'

'She asked me if I lived alone and I said I lived with another woman.' Dee reached out and pulled a leaf from the apple tree: 'It's not exactly a dead give-away, I didn't think, but she went rigid for the rest of the morning and said "I see" meaningfully.'

Ann raised her eyebrows: 'It doesn't sound as if she's taking it too well. Do you think it'll make working there difficult?'

Dee folded the leaf slowly into four segments. 'I don't think so,' she said, 'I imagine that as soon as she's digested it she'll want not to talk about it, at least for a while. I don't see her interfering or anything.'

Ann looked at her over her pad: 'Bit hopeful, aren't you? Don't you want to discuss it, anyway, challenge her assumptions at all?'

She shrugged, 'When she's used to me, perhaps. She'll only think I'm a freak if I bring it up now.'

'You mean you want to appear normal.'

Dee spread the bruised leaf carefully out on the table. The sap was wet on her fingers. 'Yes,' she said, 'I do, I suppose — human. Then maybe she'll be able to listen to me. It's really the only way.'

Ann was silent for a time, bent over in her chair. 'It seems to me like denying who you are,' she said finally. 'But maybe you're right. I wish we didn't have to treat the world so gently. Here —' she tossed a page across the table, 'what d'you think?'

Dee picked up the paper, it was a picture of her sitting cross-legged, her shirt a billowing red. 'Hey, I look flamboyant —' she grinned: 'How come my shirt gets to be coloured and the rest of me's in pencil — does that mean the rest of me doesn't exist?'

'I've told you you don't understand art.' Ann rocked back in her chair, 'I could give it a title, "Dee in a red shirt", d'you see?'

'Yes, or it could have another title, "Dee in the shirt that Ann covets most".'

Ann laughed and waved her arms in the air: 'But that shirt is a metaphor for your most charming, your most worthwhile, your most rewarding characteristics! Of course I want all those, or what am I here for?'

* * * * * * * * * * * * * *

At first Eleanor wanted to close the shop as soon as Dee left, to close the door and pull down the blinds and pace behind them where no one could come at her. But she found she was afraid of letting go like that; she did not want to start to think quite yet. Better to carry through the routine, to keep to it. She might need it. There were not many customers during the afternoon; in the intervals of serving Eleanor walked about the shop attending minutely to the displays, laboriously ensuring that each box on view was full, that piles and heaps of fruit were symmetrical. There was a solitary late shopper who appeared as she was finally closing — she let her in — it was no trouble, there was no hurry. When she too was gone Eleanor drove the bolts home, tumbled the blinds into their places and looked round: a corner of the newspaper in the window had slipped. She crossed the floor and replaced it. Then she left the shop and climbed the stairs.

The cat was in her usual place; when Eleanor bent and picked her up she purred, and dribbled. Eleanor stood over the cat while she ate, thinking that she would wash the plate straight away, as soon as the cat had finished. It was as well to have everything out of the way. She realised that she was still wearing her overall; she glanced down — the cat seemed to be eating slowly and had still some food left — so she turned and went back down the stairs to the shop. She hung the overall on a peg and brought the cigarettes out of the pocket. There was really no point going back upstairs — she would go out into the garden.

But outside the sun was shining, it was a fine evening. Her neighbours on either side were gathering, she could see them, on their striped chairs. Out there she might at any moment have to talk to them, they might sing out at any moment. Eleanor stepped back inside the back door — where was she to go? Not the shop, dark and deserted at this time, like a mausoleum with its contents all covered, shrouded for the night. It would have to be her front room — where else was she thinking of going, after all.

Eleanor climbed once more; the paint was flaking off the banisters again, it seemed to happen so quickly, had she knocked it with something? She paused at the top — the cat's saucer. It would give her something to do later on. She turned into the front room: 'Why are you so upset?' she said aloud, to the room. But there was no surprising it into retreat like that, what had come out after all this time.

Dee had made her remember. She had thought that there was nothing to remember —nothing that she didn't know. But Dee, sitting opposite, hunched up in that way she had, smiling to herself, saying that she lived with another woman — it was outrageous, it was insane, who did she think she was? Things were different, of course — things you couldn't dream of then, taken for granted now. What would it have been like, then? They never found out, that was the worst of it. And here was this child taking it all on — for it couldn't really be so very different, she knew — with that secret smile.

Eleanor found that she was smoking, that she was grinding a butt into the ashtray. She stared down at her hand, let the butt fall. Had she held on to herself all day to let out only this rush of hatred for Dee and her friend, for lightly, ignorantly doing something she knew to be impossible? They could live together, of course, perhaps things were different enough for that, think that they were free to do it. They thought they could do anything. But they would find that the will to do it wasn't enough. The physical conditions weren't enough, either. They could set up home together, everything as they wanted it — and it wouldn't work. They'd find that out — or they might not, might just blame each other and go off and do it somewhere else. But sooner or later they'd have to realise that it wasn't allowed, that if they would go on in that track obstacles would be set up all round them. No one would believe in them. They'd lose faith in themselves.

She paced the length of the room, her hands clasped about her body; in the middle of the room she wheeled off to the window and looked down into the street — there were a few boys making towards the pub, shouting to each other, bumping casually against the brick wall opposite.

She was afraid, that was it, supposing it were still worth it, even if it wasn't perfect, supposing it were better than nothing? Oh, but — she mouthed the words to herself, raising her hands and shrugging at the window — but how go for something just because it ought to be perfection, knowing it has everything working against it, that it must come out a mess, a betrayal, no different from anything else? She turned from the window. But I wanted it, I wanted it, it was worth it because it was just that I wanted — the refrain sprung out at her without warning. In her head the words sounded plaintive, a thin hopeless wail; she saw herself small, arms wrapped round her knees, rocking backwards and forwards, inconsolable, hugging misery. She began to speak, to block out the sound.

'Very useful, very very useful.' She stared round the room. 'Supper. You haven't had supper.'

In the kitchen she took two eggs from the box and cracked them into a bowl. Perhaps these, Dee and the other, didn't care that there would be nothing lasting? It was as good a way as any to pass the time, companionship, warm flesh in the bed, giving out heat — was that all it meant now, a casual arrangement, mutual convenience, not much given on either side? Eleanor grimaced as she stirred blobs of butter into the eggs, perhaps it hardly mattered to them, that they were two women? Naive enough to think they were immune from taboo, were they? She paused, lifting the cheese grater down from the shelf; no, she thought, Dee is not like that, holds herself in, away, she's wary of the world. Knows she departs from it somewhere. Eleanor brought the grater down onto the chopping board and picked up the cheese, I must not hate her so for doing it, she thought. I chose not to. I chose not, because it would not have been good enough.

Smooth swirls of cheese piled onto the board. To go against everything, how sure you have to be. And we were not, she thought, we were not; Bea — oh, I could perhaps have persuaded her, but how should we have lived with that? She held her hand over the pan; a little cool yet. It was an odd attitude, of course, how was anything done without compromise, without knowing you were bound to fail at least in part — the mixture coursed across the pan — but that was just an empty phrase, she thought, lifting the edges of the omelette, swilling butter round, the possibility of Bea only was there if it was going to be different from what else there was, quite different. Otherwise better get married, or not, make do as others did. The omelette slid onto the plate. What was there in it for Dee, then? Did she really not want to live with a man, could it seem worth bothering, just for that? But she's in love, no doubt, she thought. Thinks it will triumph. That sort of childhood, no experience of obstacles that stay in your way. She carried the folded omelette through into the front room; it comes to the same in the end, her hope and my foresight. And poor Dee, she thought, she has to try and live up to it.

The fork cut cleanly through the omelette. This plate, one of her mother's. Did she remember right? A market stall somewhere, canvas awnings, wet khaki. Her shoes leaking, darkening her socks. Ma stopping with a little grunt, jerking some dirty bit of china out: 'Look, Nellie, this'll

60

do, better than the one we broke last week.' Trying not to look at it, either of them, at the bright flowers. Or was that something else, another time, a flowery dress, 'This'll do nicely, Nellie.' Both of them trying not to look. An ugly plate. She knew how to make do. That was the trouble — all too well. Cut your losses, stand back, conserve your strength. Those that reached out after something, after all, where did they end but by making do? There was no point, she had seen that too many times; just so many ways of playing out disappointment.

There is no need, thought Eleanor, walking back to the kitchen, no need to have done it all directly. Plenty of others' experiences: expecting, waiting, being disappointed — she had seen and heard enough about that. Who really needs to experience the boredom of washing-up, she thought, the green bubbles in the bowl — who needs to stand by a sink daily with the piles of plates stacked up on both sides, pink rubber gloves clinging to your clammy hands? The boredom of washing-up, the ecstasy of love, the boredom of love. I know enough of that. I did not need to drag my body through it, filling in the details — this is how Bea looks with her hair wet from the bath; this is how Bea looks when she has lost an argument; this is how I feel, seeing her across the street.

She stooped suddenly to pick up the cat's saucer. Not quite proof against that. Partly that was the problem — she did want memories. Ridiculous, to refuse to live for the moment, that dragging yourself through everything — and to come out at the end finding yourself longing for memories. Eleanor dried her hands. The kitchen window looked out over the yard and a triangle of neighbour's garden. In the triangle showed yellow roses — old blooms, their petals littering the ground. A woman crossed the patch carrying a striped chair back towards the house, her other hand clutching an open book, yellow, a detective story from the library. No doubt we should have sat stolidly in the garden reading detective stories, Eleanor thought. Perhaps having Bea I should not have read all that I have, should have read detective stories instead. Memories instead of information. Neither is worth much, she thought. Both being distractions, only that experience and memories have more lies and more hope.

She climbed to the bathroom, opened the window, turned on the taps. It was early yet, for a bath; hardly dusk outside. But she did not want to sit in the front room waiting for the time to be right. Her bedroom at least was already darkening; the skylight held the light, hardly filtering it. Eleanor dropped her clothes in a small heap. How easy it is, she thought, to shed that skin; these are not layers that cling, they hang loose and drop

61

quickly. Even my knickers are loose, fall in a moment. They do not pause on a hip bone or notice my knees as they fall. How simple to be free of these, and how I am wrapped like a thick blanket in wanting, never to be sloughed off. Itchy and demanding, coarse, noisy, whispering on about how good this might have been, or that, how exciting. How it's always worth trying. And underneath I am thin and white and my skin is cold and wrinkled. I do not need a blanket.

A blanket that cries in the night, 'It is never too late', its shrieks of discontent are supposed to tell me that I am alive, part of the human race still, a prey to everywoman's needs. How pleasant finally to be able to cast it off and step away, wrinkled lizard body comfortable under a familiar stone.

She grimaced, still standing over the pile of clothing; she did not want to be some stone-headed beast guided by tedious, mysterious instinct. Only to be rid of this itch. The same contrary thorn that would never quite listen to reason, its arguments childishly simple, who often said only, 'Well, you can't be sure, can you?' or 'It might have been worth it for its own sake, just for that.' And when she said, 'You're a child of your time,' it would always say, 'I'm your child.'

In the bathroom the bath had run warm. The room itself was warm and still, the heat of the day lying there under the roof. Eleanor lay in the water and watched the colours of the sunset fall on the wall opposite the window. Why was it that seeing that pink light on the wall, her body in the water, made her think of being a child? There was no bathroom at home, of course, might have been someone else's she went to once. That was it; some girl and her family had offered to take her along on holiday. That was where there was a bath, the sun setting on a wall. And somehow ma had given her spending money and she'd not been able to spend it, thinking how much more they needed it at home. Only at the last moment a stick of rock to bring back to remember it all by. And ma had been angry, after all, when she came back with it. That was what I gave it to you for. I gave it to you. She kept saying. Sitting at the kitchen table for hours that night clinging to the stick of rock, over and over, 'I bought the rock, ma — look, I bought the rock.' What had she expected.

Eleanor lay on in the water, looking down over her body. A neglected body, she thought, by some standards. Not subjected to much treatment for its preservation, and wrinkled in all the expected places, runnels of loose skin gathering between the breasts, hanging over the knees, braceleted round the neck. As if it thinks it might be going somewhere, might run off and away, Eleanor thought, watching water collect and spill at her navel. She stood up carefully with the soap. There seemed to be always the same problem, the desire to get rid of something coming up against rigidity. Her skin would not melt. She could not spend her spending money. She could not rid herself quite of Bea, of that tiresome niggling faith in possibility. Rigidity.

Who can say why pubic hair goes grey first? Or, she thought, is it just mine? That would not be so difficult to interpret. Grey hairs death's blossom. She stepped out of the bath. All this had been going on too long, she felt suddenly, her mind too would be growing grey hairs in a minute from the tedium of it all, always thinking the same thoughts. She put on her dressing-gown. What now, she thought, going through the motions of preparing for bed, reaching for the hairbrush — but not, somehow, quite ready. Not this stalemate, not again — perhaps I could send Bea something anonymous through the post for her birthday.

Eleanor giggled, finding herself going back down the stairs. An old bit of Devon rock done up in ribbon. She walked down the corridor into the kitchen; there was the plate she had eaten her omelette off this evening, upright in the dish-rack.

In the dusk the pattern was dim. Eleanor smiled and picked up the plate. Her feet were bare, but that was the kind of detail, she thought, that she would let go now. She went on down the stairs and out of the back door. It was almost dark; no one was out in the gardens on either side. They would be at the front now, in their warm front rooms. The concrete of the yard, and then the grass cold on her feet. She went on down the length of the garden to the bonfire, where she burnt broken crates and cardboard when the dustbins overflowed. She put the plate down at the edge of the scorched earth.

We always hated this plate, both of us. And I've been keeping it for the last fifteen years. She picked up a big stone from the flower bed. This is for you, ma, for having to make do. For me having to make do.

She dropped the stone onto the centre of the plate, cracking it across. She picked it up again and threw it down: the plate broke, each half splintering into shards. She stared down.

Afterwards she lay for a long time on top of her bed in her dressing-gown, looking up at the skylight. It was soothing that the darkness thickened gradually as the night wore away, the yellow tint fading as the village's few street lights flicked out.

In the morning it rained. Dee was caught on the way to the shop, a heavy shower that flattened her hair and beat into her sweater. She stopped at the shop doorway and swept her fringe out of her eyes; the door was on the latch and she slipped through and began the business of readying the store for opening time.

Eleanor came through from the back.

'Did you have a coat?'

Dee shook her head, 'But there was very little rain.'

Eleanor peered across the room, dark with the clouds passing over. 'You'd better turn the lights on,' she said, 'I'll be down in a minute.'

Dee crossed to the switch; she did not know how to begin to get around the barrier between them, now that it was suddenly there, there because of yesterday. So Eleanor had not liked what she'd found out. Dee realised how much she'd been hoping, taking for granted, that Eleanor would not close off from her. But it was going to be like this. She didn't, when it came to it, know how to confront this cold hostility. She stared out of the window and dug her hands into her armpits; it would be best to leave. She turned at Eleanor's tread on the stairs.

'Here,' Eleanor came across the room, a bundle in her hand, 'you'd better put on this jersey of mine, and let that one dry off somewhere. You'll catch cold.'

Dee grasped the woolly lump gratefully.

'You can hang it upstairs in the kitchen, there's a line.'

Dee ran upstairs, the warm rough sleeves of Eleanor's sweater rubbing her damp hands; it was going to be all right, then. Speech, at least.

Eleanor watched her walking about the shop, hunched into the jersey that on her came half-way to her knees. She watched Dee carry it about with her, a warming talisman. Saw how she lightened, wearing it. Difficult to ignore that vulnerability. No need, really, to stand off. What she wanted to know could as well be found out from a little closer.

They stood together to serve the customers, an assembly line. Dee's eyes trailed over the customers' faces, the hooks of brown bags hanging on the wall, across the wooden slats of the floor to the vegetables — was it the potatoes she was wanting, peas? — dragged to the till, the door, lifted to follow a back, coated against the cold, over the threshold. Beside her Eleanor spun fruit in bags, meeting these women half-way, anticipating, each gesture an economy of movement, from box to bag. She stood and smiled and drew them off, her sharp smile defying indecision.

They stood for a moment in the first silence.

'Have you lived together long, you and your friend?' she asked.

Asking for confirmation, Dee thought, a formality. Going to make something of permanence, though, is she? Dee fingered the cuff of the jersey, 'We've only been in the country together six months,' this is not a battle, she thought, she has leant you her sweater, 'in the city much longer, but we didn't live in the same house, then.'

'You came out here for that?'

Perhaps they all did. Eleanor looked at Dee, rolling and unrolling her cuff. How pathetic that they should all make this tangible, futile gesture of escape. Getting away from the world, to find it as much here as anywhere. They leave you alone here, but that's not tolerance.

'We came for a host of reasons, it's a little difficult —' Dee eyed the gap between them, gathered herself for it: 'I suppose you could say we're refugees from the ghetto.'

She felt better, on such ground, even if she was exaggerating, even if she was incomprehensible. At least, for a moment, she had said more than she had been asked. 'In London, we lived in houses with other women. Our friends, you see. And then there were other houses — it was very active, took up a great deal of energy, just being there.'

Dee walked across the floor, away from Eleanor. She stopped over a box of pears and bent down, picking the fruit up in her hand, turning it, replacing it.

'There was too much personal life,' she spoke over her shoulder, 'that never went anywhere. We have a slogan, the women's movement, 'the personal is political' — means that we start from our personal experience and from that build a theory of the world, a political theory.' She paused. The skin of the green speckled pears was stiff, thin, glossy. 'We began to have no time for the theories, there. Analysis stopped in the next bed, the next room, house politics —' She turned round: 'I never went out. Just sat in the house all day and talked, not about the world any more, you see. About us. How we should live. It began to seem unreal.'

Dee leaned back against the crate, of course the gap was unbridgeable, she could hardly conjure up that house. She almost did not want to, why expose it to this woman who would not understand, who would only grasp things. The multi-coloured banisters, the lists in the kitchen. Vegetable stews and the dole, she might have seen it on the box, as a category, just another style, arbitrary choice one or another. Something you passed through. Dee turned again, bending over the pears, a customer had come in, let Eleanor deal with her. She wished to take back what she had said, to begin somewhere else. The shop door closed again.

She said: 'Not that I don't believe in all that as necessary. I'll go back to it, I suppose. It was a particular time, we'd all given up something — not just our jobs, I mean, we'd given up participating outside. It had become too alien. We had no effect out there. We'd all withdrawn, were waiting for where it would be possible to do something next. Some new opening.'

Dee felt herself speaking across a growing distance, Eleanor across the floor a thin shadow. What did she know of this person? What were these words meaning to her, these few odd words. I am trying to describe, she thought, a group of women alienated from their culture, so alienated that we are always trying to identify new assumptions we have from it, root them out. But that is something you can only experience, the point is to experience it, not to describe it. There is no point in a description.

'No one was listening to us,' she said.

Eleanor drew a stool out from the back room and sat down. 'You don't expect me to understand.' She took out a cigarette, dropped the spent match to the floor. She would sweep later. She cupped a hand under her elbow and looked over at Dee who stood at the other side of the room. One story is the same as another.

'Tell me about your friend.'

'About Ann?'

Dee waved her hand, pushing that aside. Another random, partial description, it was useless, another empty gesture. Eleanor sitting there, these questions nipping out of her; it was like being drained of blood, of energy. As if all substance were being sucked out of her until she were translucent, a jellyfish. Weak at the knees.

'I don't know what you want to hear,' she said. 'Ask her yourself. She's coming in for some food before lunch. She'll tell you, she's more loquacious than me.'

Dee stood stiffly, still across the breadth of the room; it was an intrusion, Ann forcing herself in like this. She would come, she would make herself felt — it was a matter of principle, she said, that Eleanor should not be able to ignore her — but she could go away again, too. And I shall have to put up with Eleanor feeling that she is having things thrust upon her, thought Dee, damn them both.

'I don't quite understand the necessity for a crusade,' Eleanor said quietly, watching smoke rise towards the ceiling.

'Oh, ask Ann that as well.' Dee thrust her hands into her pockets and turned to watch the street. Eleanor finished her cigarette and carried the stool back into the back room.

They both saw Ann when she came up the street, dressed in black, a red scarf round her neck. Eleanor knew her at once, perhaps because that way of dressing did not match the preoccupations of other young women in the village. Perhaps because Dee stiffened, standing at the window.

Ann came into the shop smiling; at the sight of her Dee saw that her temper was ridiculous, childish, rude. She began to explain, gesturing between Ann and Eleanor. She must make it up to them both. 'Hello Ann — this is Ann, Eleanor. I've been trying to explain us, why we're here. I don't do us very well.'

Ann grinned at Eleanor, 'What has she been saying about me?'

'Nothing. She refused to describe you.'

'And us?'

'A rather confusing explanation for your being here.'

Ann glanced between them, was it wise to pursue this alliance, she wondered, to come between them like this?

But Dee shrugged, 'Why not give your version — I've already said you're loquacious.' It was enough that she could use Ann to placate Eleanor; she had so nearly overstepped a line of safety. She wanted to go on here.

'Well,' Ann drew a tobacco packet out of her pocket, began to roll a cigarette, both hands for a moment full with papers and packet, then the packet stowed away, the cigarette rolled, sealed, lit. She inhaled: 'Well, in the lesbian feminist ghetto,' she looked at the ceiling, how good it was to come out with, 'the current idea is that multiple relationships are a necessary part of the life-style.' She grinned at the space between Eleanor and Dee, 'Now, I think that would be very nice. Ideal, even. Because of course monogamy as now practised has its many evils.'

'You can put ash on the floor,' said Eleanor, 'I have to sweep anyway.'

Ann paused over her cigarette, flicking ash, 'At the moment, though, it seems impossible to achieve. Certainly if you have anything else to do. So we opted for lonely depth, out here.' She glanced over at Dee: 'For a while, anyway. I simplify, of course.'

'You don't exactly explain, either.' Dee struggled for some phrase that would show up her own need, to have something solid to base herself on.

'Why "ghetto"?' Eleanor asked in that morning's still tone. She leant at the till, not watching either of them.

'Because we're different enough for it to be necessary. And because we don't want to be integrated into a society we don't want to support.' Dee spoke abruptly, conscious of her words as angular, without Ann's elegance. But it was immediate, without Ann's layer of irony that so neatly distanced her from their politics, their beliefs. As if Ann were open to adopting something more civilised, should Eleanor only suggest it.

'It's a community,' Ann's hands shaped the air in front of her, 'a necessary support system, as Dee says. It provides us with what identity we have. But because the world in general and we as well — unconsciously perhaps, but still — because its values are always being devalued —'

'I know about theories of ghettoisation.' Eleanor's gesture arrested Ann's movement, caught describing a circle before her, 'But it seems like a mistake to me. You should be trying to make your place in the world. What future is there outside it?' Mere playing at victims, she thought, working at molehills until they blocked out the view.

'But of course we want a place —' Dee stopped — this all seemed quite out of control, all three of them snarling in corners. And there was Ann, wearing her favourite scarf and clean trousers, her presentable self put on specially. And here she was, wearing Eleanor's jersey, wearing it fulsomely. And Eleanor had given it to her. Was that all it was to be, gestures of good-will, nothing more solid than misunderstanding underneath? Papering over chasms.

'Time for my tea.' Eleanor stood up and went out towards the kitchen.

'Does that mean I should go?' Ann whispered.

'Not necessarily. Wait and see how many cups she puts on the tray.'

'Christ.'

'Can't you turn on the charm a little, Ann?'

'You can see, I'm trying — but she thinks I'm frivolous.'

'And middle-class.'

Ann shrugged, rolling another cigarette: 'Well, I am.'

'You know very well — you don't have to come on like a lecturer.'

'I should just accept the impossibility of communication.'

Someone had come into the shop. Dee turned, smiling: 'Can I help you?'

In the kitchen Eleanor spooned tea into the larger tea-pot. I should use the other one, they'll be having a second cup out of this. What is this going on in my shop? She looked at the row of mugs on the shelf — hadn't I better drive them out, sitting down there? Two of them, together. It'll have to be done some time; do they think I want anything to do with them? She put the three mugs on the tray. Not a molehill, of course it wasn't. And they would be better off together, lots of them together, perhaps that was how they believed things. She bent to fill the cat's saucer; there's no room for me, she thought, that's it, I don't like being excluded. An exclusive ghetto for the young. The young eat biscuits — she put her hand to the packet — I eat biscuits too, no one makes general-isations about that, the middle-aged, spinsters, eat biscuits. No one feels they ought to worry about whether they eat biscuits, the old must buy their own biscuits. Build their own ghettos. Ghettos — what do I want with a ghetto — too late for that. An old people's home, more like. She carried the tray down the stairs; a customer was just leaving the shop. On either side of the door the two turned towards her, both small suddenly across the length of the floor, turning warily at the sound of her footsteps. Like, she thought, nervous animals.

Ann sidled over: 'Three mugs.'

'I know about politeness as well as ghettos.'

Dee, watching them, noticed that they both had their heads slightly at an angle, as if judging a distance. 'There are extra chairs,' she said loudly, moving across the room, as if she were trying to cut the line of sight drawn between the two women with her voice. 'They're in the back, I'll get them.' She came back with the chairs, quickly. They were still standing like that, getting a bead on each other.

'If it's just politeness,' Ann said.

But Eleanor turned suddenly, running a hand through her hair, and seized the chairs from Dee. She put them down close together, fetched her stool and sat down on it between the chairs. 'No, it's not,' she grinned, 'I'm genuinely interested in interrogating you.'

Ann sat down, 'Can I really put my ash on the floor?'

'Of course — and then you can sweep the floor afterwards.'

Ann laughed: 'Sure.'

'I'll pour the tea, shall I.' Dee began to measure out milk carefully; both of them needed to have their tea right, or they'd be upset again. She struggled with the cellophane on the biscuit packet. Now she was nursing them both. It had been Ann's idea to come along, she could get herself out, then. She'd only come thinking she could get away with it, come because she thought she could charm Eleanor out of the trees. Like she could everyone else. Not really because, it was the thing to do, to confront Eleanor.

'I can't open the damn biscuits,' Dee said. How tiring it was, trying to bring your politics into your life. And how boring for other people.

'I have a penknife,' Ann proffered.

'I've done it with my teeth now.' Dee slumped into her chair, took three biscuits from the packet, and settled back to eat them, her mug clutched to her chest.

Gone into hibernation, thought Eleanor. That glazed munching look. She turned to look at Ann, small and sharp-edged in her chair. Easy enough to imagine needing to get away from that, those sharp digging elbows. But not conclusive: plenty of weak minds in sharp little bodies. All the same if she were fatter, she thought, I'd think her less sharp. She knows she starts with that advantage, Eleanor realised, watching the neat movements of Ann's hands as she rolled another cigarette.

'You don't work,' she said.

'Yes I do.' Ann paused to lick the gummed paper, eyed Eleanor over the lifted cigarette: 'I paint, draw, sculpt. I am an artist, you could say.' She lit up, 'I don't make any money to speak of.'

'Do people not like your stuff, then?' Eleanor grinned. She was enjoying riling this child, who could make Dee feel dumb and plodding. Here I am now, fighting other people's battles, she thought suddenly, a mistake. Just look, Nellie, no need to see with your hands.

'They mostly don't see it. There's nowhere to show near here.' Ann admired the regularity of the argument, each question and answer complete, no more than necessary, yet leading on to the next.

'Would they like it if they did see it?'

Ann grinned, she had expected that one: 'I try to make my work accessible.'

Eleanor took a biscuit from the packet, examined it, 'Is that difficult?'

Christ. Ann buried her head in her mug for a moment. Talk about throwing down the goddam gauntlet. She said finally, drawing out the words: 'I do sometimes find that there is a conflict between my personal idea of something and a form of it that will come across to other people, yes. But I also think that my personal experience and work as a woman is of direct relevance to other women, and that my work, when it succeeds, speaks to them.'

Eleanor nibbled a corner of her biscuit. She did not speak, seeing Ann trembling on the edge of rage. How quickly they both fired up, how near the surface they seemed to live. Thinking that, she said, 'I'd like to see the things you do.'

Ann looked at her blankly for a moment, 'Of course, you must come out some time. An early closing day, perhaps, for the light.' Ann recovered herself: 'You shall say whether they are accessible, since you don't trust me to know.'

Eleanor nodded vaguely. She had forgotten for a moment that they did not know of what she somehow seemed to think of as the connection between herself and them. That they were doing something she once thought she might. They did not know, either, that to her they were specimens that she wanted to inspect for similarities, differences to herself twenty-five years ago. Would she and Bea have come to the same thing? And what was it they had come to? But she wasn't going to go after them at a run with the net held ready, to pursue them. And yet these two were spreading their own nets. Thinking her a worthy prey, middle-aged and wearing a nylon overall. Why was that? Just because she was those things, all an overall-wearer should be. The woman in the street. One of those they wanted to reach out to, no doubt, with their paintings and theories.

'I can't guarantee to represent everywoman, you know.'

'I would be interested to have your personal opinion.'

I certainly shall not go, thought Eleanor, let them propagandise somewhere else.

Dee reached out for the biscuits: 'Perhaps you should try and put something on in the village, Ann. The church hall or the W.I.' She tore clumsily at the seams of the packet, 'I'm afraid I'm eating too many biscuits.'

Ann gazed at Dee taking herself another handful, going back to sleep. Throwing in the W.I. Hoping no doubt that she'd fall happily in, scoffing at Women's Institutes, and let Eleanor finish her off. Because of the work, that's it, she doesn't like to hear me talk about it. Thinks I make too much of it. I seem to spend my entire time among people who don't believe in what I'm doing. It takes all my energy to persuade them for half-an-hour that I'm not completely insane and wasting my life. Please Dee, won't you sit for me. Please Eleanor won't you agree to differ on my work, my politics, my life-style. A running dialogue with moderation, surely it's not feminist to paint just me, I'm your lover. Surely if you must be a lesbian,

71

there's no need to advertise it. No need to live with others like that. No need to pretend you like it. No need to sit here.

Ann stood up, 'I'd better get along. Let me know when you're coming, Eleanor.'

In the shop Dee finished her biscuit.

'Did she have the vegetables she wanted?' Eleanor asked.

'Oh, yes. I did them while you were making the tea. We've paid.' Eleanor poured more tea, 'She went rather abruptly.'

Dee still sat huddled over her cup, her eyes elsewhere: 'Yes, she did, didn't she.'

'Do you know why?' Eleanor watched Dee focus on the floor for a while, considering this.

'One of us drove her away,' she said.

'You don't think she just went?'

Dee smiled across at Eleanor, pleased with this careful inquisition: 'I don't think she liked either of us today.'

Ann was outside, carrying her haversack. At the corner she stopped to put it on, to roll another cigarette. She looked at her watch, too late for anything but going home and starting the lunch. The vegetables in the haversack dug into her back. Defeated by marrows. She started off on the road out of the village.

The rain still lay on the hedges. Ann stopped at a gate, laying her arms along the sodden wood. A rough field, high with thistles, sloped away to what was probably a stream or a ditch. On the other side the ground rose more steeply to a ridge blotted with a clump of trees. There had been hay in the further field; a few bales were scattered about the hill. Ann reached into her pocket for her tobacco. Smoking too much today, she thought, rolling a cigarette. Look at this landscape, just look at it. Lacks all merit. Vague slope, half a stream and a messy hill. Put in the gate – Ann stepped back across the road – only makes it more conventional. She leant on the gate, I could paint this lot, any number of styles. An English landscape. Ah yes they would cry the rolling English countryside. Our gentle beauty. Call it a boring English landscape, they would think I was subverting an entire culture. Of course I couldn't paint it as boring as it really is, thistles, a ditch and midges. And low cloud, there's a name for that too, a rainy day in summer by Miss Ann Fleming. Price £15 or two bunches of fresh-picked scones. Oh shit. Ann walked on, stopped to pick a buttercup and thrust the stalk through the front of her jersey. A decent colour at least. An arrangement from the hedgerow. No good getting at them. I know, I know. Easy targets hated by the rest of the world. Full of strong women, all that.

She had reached the gate, the little garden gate that should be brightly painted and welcoming. She flung it to behind her. Domestication everywhere, domesticated women and domesticated landscape. The whole country inches thick under a layer of civilisation. We don't exhibit things like that at the W.I. We don't exhibit that kind of thing at all. What would my husband say. Ann unloaded the haversack onto the kitchen table and brought out the chopping board. Yuck, he would say, erk. Or was that too extreme. Not quite my sort of thing, our sort of thing. Ann realised that she was about to cry. She moved the chopping board out towards the middle of the table. Nobody was going to eat her tears for lunch. Here I am, she thought, neatly chopping vegetables, screaming to myself fuck moderation fuck compromise fuck accessibility. I go on peaceably making lunch. When Dee comes in I shall not turn on her with the knife for deserting me in the shop this morning. I shall not put the knife in my haversack and walk back to the shop and run Eleanor through for refusing to believe in me as a person with a contribution to make to the world. Not only am I not going to react with any decent vigour to these betrayals, I am not going to pack my belongings and go looking for wild women and wild landscapes. I am not even going to stop making the lunch, why is that. As bound as any other housewife by other people's expectations. Why didn't you make the lunch dear. Isn't that a little unreasonable. It's not much to ask after all. Except that Dee would make more of an effort to understand. Would be good-humoured, make the lunch herself. And expect to be told what was the matter. All the same in the end, it's less trouble to make the lunch. There you are – compromise, moderation. Ann set the pan on the stove, adjusted the heat, found a lid that fitted, swept the vegetable parings into the compost bucket. She went out towards the garden, remembered that the grass would be wet, turned and climbed the stairs to her room.

The women at the bus stop painting stood against the wall. She propped it up on the desk and looked at it. A line of women, grim, drawn, make-up like a taunt, an obscene graffiti, on limp cheeks. Accessible enough, you would have thought. I think I'll put myself in at the back there, join the freak show, we're all in it together. But I've made them look too human, who can be human and female, what chance? And that three-dimensional look, a mockery. A series of cardboard cut-outs we all are, should be able to see the struts at the back, holding us up in a neat line. Just cut me out and look, I fit in. Kitchen sink too low? Cut off her feet. This painting is all wrong, going for naturalism. Gives them an out, someone else standing at the bus stop, not me. Even if I put the queen at the head of the queue. Make them cardboard, the struts showing, propped at the bus stop. That's how it is. To hell with them, that's not real, she's being extreme.

Ann eyed the painting for a while. She took hold of a knife, traced out lines in the air, that part would have to come off, and that. She put the knife aside. So you don't trust yourself when you're angry. Think it may be affecting your judgement. Art in tranquillity, the emotion tempered, all that shit. She sat down on the edge of the bed. Have another cigarette, instant tranquillity. She looked around the room for an ashtray. There was a saucer on the floor by her feet. She dropped the match into it, put it on the chair next to the bed.

I never swept the shop floor, she thought. But I'm not going to think about them now. She looked at her watch — half-an-hour before lunch would be ready, before Dee would be back. She swung her legs up onto the bed and lay back, blowing smoke towards the ceiling. Compromise, moderation. Clearly it was not worth her while knifing Dee or Eleanor. She didn't really want to. And lunch, there was not much mileage to be had out of not making lunch. It wouldn't get her anywhere. There were more direct ways of voicing protest, she could quite well bring up Dee's behaviour in the shop and they would talk about it. No need to resort to inarticulate thrusts. Neither of those impulses represented what she wanted, a good enough reason for moderation. But then there was the desire to leave.

Ann stared at the white ceiling, fixedly at a small patch above her where the plaster was uneven and a rough lump cast a shadow. For that was not so easy to think about. She felt the fear —was it excitement? starting; her stomach seeming to contract and her mind contracting in concert. Thick walls coming in around, so that she heard in her head only the same question: 'Do I want to go?'

The walls would not give enough for her to find a way to an answer. Except, she thought, this performance probably means I do. She lay rigid, feeling her brain paralysed. She would never be able to think about this, it

74

was always the same, too hard to face. She started in and her brain seized up. There were too many things to think about at once. They all had to be weighed up.

Supposing she said, of course I am staying here with Dee, nothing has happened to change that commitment. That is not compromise, that is trying to do something thoroughly. You could say it was an immoderate commitment. I will complain about today, we will talk about Eleanor. The decision made.

But then there's the landscape, the people, so limp and flattening. In the city at least there is ugliness, other women. And I am alone, there is no one who sees what I am trying to do − why pretend otherwise. Why pretend a common purpose. Why waste all this time persuading here and there. I could go and get on with what I'm doing and let them have it at the end, take it or leave it. Ann sat up − she could do that here, after all. Lead an immoderate life in the country. An immoderate life in the country.

She glanced over at the painting on the desk, stood up and carried it over to face the wall. Her next would be so inaccessible; she grinned, running down the stairs. Not abstract, but obscurely representational. A picture of some banisters. Or some miniature banisters in wood. Called, say, radical feminist series 4. That would get Eleanor. She would look at it, her head on one side and say, 'Everywoman's banisters?' or perhaps, 'Do you polish them every week?'

Ann took the lid off the vegetables and stirred, a little too watery. She turned the heat up; I have started to take her into account, she thought, as if she is going to come into our lives. A middle-aged woman who thinks I'm arrogant and middle-class. And who of course thinks lesbians are freaks. Who certainly have nothing to say to the rest of the world. They should be trying to integrate themselves. Who needs any more like that, Eleanors telling us to keep quiet − why are we inviting her in as if we wanted to hear it? You're not telling me we're going to change her mind about much. Ann put forks on the table, perhaps Dee will spread the word, smiling at customers over the bananas. This could be your daughter. Or your sister. Not your mother, there was that − being only the two of them they didn't cover the age-range so well. Probably no loss at the moment. Let them get used to daughters.

* * * * * * * * * * * * * * *

Bea could see the flash of her red shorts at the other side of the fruit-cage, the green of her top disappearing into the leaves of the red currant bushes. 'We have to finish off one bush before going on to the next one,' she called.

Nell came over and squatted down, her hands diving into Bea's gooseberry bush, 'Why? I can just as well pick them all at once.'

'Because that way none of them ever get picked properly. Half the fruit gets left.'

Nell shuffled round, reaching for the ripest gooseberries hanging underneath the bush, close to the ground. 'Not necessarily,' she said, 'you can be selective about the kind of fruit you want to pick. You can leave the unripe stuff for later and the small stuff for when you want to make jam.''

'And I shall end up with six bushes to pick instead of one.' Bea drew off her gloves: 'If you're going to pick the gooseberries you'd better put these on, or you'll get scratched.'

Nell shook her head: 'It doesn't hurt.' She sat back for a moment, a handful on the ground beside her, watching her mother take a cigarette out of the packet in her gardening apron. 'You should stop smoking, mum. It's bad for you.'

Bea shrugged, 'I know.'

Nell sat in silence, topping and tailing fat red gooseberries. She began to eat them, the smallest first. 'You never listen to anything I say, do you.'

'Of course I do.' Bea reached a strand of red currants from a basket. 'But I decide to smoke all the same. Like you decide not to wear gloves for the gooseberries, although you get scratched.'

'I don't get lung cancer from gooseberry scratches.'

'It's the same principle.'

'If you were aware of the risks, really aware of them, you wouldn't smoke. You go on doing it by closing your eyes and pretending it won't happen to you.'

'That's your father's theory.' Bea, watching the blue smoke curl upwards in the still air, wondered if it were true, that she simply blinded herself. She did not see herself dying, that certainly was true. Not with Nell only twelve. There was another ten years or so that she had to be around, to see the girls through. So at fifty or so she might go; but would the cancer bother, she wondered, to get rid of her? Not then, when nobody would really be greatly troubled by it, surely. So she ought to be worried about its coming now while she felt still needed, while she didn't want to let go. He's right in a way, Bea thought, I still do think of myself as invincible. 'I'm sure I won't get it for another ten years. It takes a long time to build up.'

'And after that?' Nell clutched her last gooseberry. If she would only stop smoking it wouldn't be just ten years. She knew quite well where this was going. Was it her fault if her mother didn't have any interests?

'It won't matter so much. You'll be grown-up.'

Nell dug into the hard earth next to her with her nail. She would not be blamed. 'I want to live past fifty,' she said angrily.

Bea finished her cigarette and buried the stub in a tuft of grass, 'I expect I shall too, when it comes to it.' And perhaps I shall, she thought. 'Why don't you try out your scientific picking theory, Nell, and we'll see how it goes — we only need about another basket for now. I'm going in to make a start with these gooseberries.'

'Ok.' Nell wandered back to the red currants. She was a little tired of picking, really. But perhaps the best from each bush; she saw a lush branch and knelt beside it. She would become a connoisseur of the art of fruit selection, as skilled as those people who spent their lives smelling perfumes, searching for the perfect rose. This was the reddest bunch. She began to search the next bush.

The kitchen buzzed with flies. Bea put her baskets on the table and sat down. The post card Ginny had sent from France lay on the chair. Bea reread the message. Sharing a dormitory and 'not having met the natives'. She turned the card over. A small chateau, not one she recognised. She remembered doing the same tour along the Loire with the family. Not long after the war. There had certainly been plenty of natives, then. She had gone to enormous lengths to meet them, sneaking out of hotels to rendezvous in hot, dimly-lit squares. How gutteral the French boys had seemed to her, and talkative, muttering and exclaiming and flinging their arms and groping in quiet streets. Urgent and exotic, exactly as expectation had painted them. She had enjoyed that holiday, it had been all she hoped for. No doubt solicitors still took their families on a tour of France, or did they? It sounded suddenly as archaic and upper-class as the grand tour. Tourism was the province of gangs of fourteen-year-olds being herded round the capitals of Europe for their education. Parents didn't feel they had to use their holidays for education any more. The middle-classes had abandoned cultural indoctrination and lay on Caribbean beaches resting against next year's heart attack. Bea took a tin basin out of a cupboard and began to top and tail the gooseberries into it. Perhaps Ginny preferred it, going with all her friends. But god knows what those teachers tell them, Bea thought, it could be anything. Whatever it is, she'll believe it. She'll come back here and tell me how the French do this or have that or are typically something. Bea's hands moved mechanically over the baskets of gooseberries. And I suppose I can't take her and show her hot squares, I used to meet young boys under that tree, that was the shop that sold the best melons for our lunches, this is what France is about for me. I could make generalisations, this is something like what Europe has always been like for the English, sex and food and energy. And comparisons: poverty of the peasant, living in the Pyrenees on slabs of dried bean puree; wealth of the middle-classes, leaving Paris each week-end for trips to the country.

Bea leant back in her chair, I couldn't tell her anything, anything she'd want to hear. She put a first lot of fruit on the stove, found the plastic bags and ties for the freezer, the chapter in the book that gave suggested cooking times, and turned back to topping and tailing. I could really go now, she thought, go out like a light, as far as they're concerned. I'm the only one that wants to stay around until I'm fifty. Crouched over the gooseberry bushes fighting off disease. Bea laughed, seeing herself. An old crone beating the air with her stick, the gooseberry bushes grown huge and thorny, cancer pacing round the fruit-cage.

She stood up again and set the first pan of gooseberries to cool. The door was kicked open in front of Nell carrying baskets of red currants. She piled them up on the draining board. Bea scooped another batch of gooseberries into the pan: 'What am I going to do with all this fruit? I'll never get rid of it.'

Nell leant up against the kitchen table, 'Yes, you will. Gooseberry fool and gooseberry tart. Gooseberry jam. Red currant jelly. And ice-cream. And frozen stuff for the winter. And summer pudding.' She paused, grinning. 'Is there any cake for tea?'

Bea looked at her watch, 'Yes, in the tin. But don't eat it all, daddy'll want some when he comes in.' She turned to light the gas under the kettle for tea.

'You could make another one before he comes home,' Nell said, her mouth full of cake.

'And ice-cream and gooseberry fool for supper. Go and empty the tea-pot, hoglet.'

Nell giggled, 'You should be glad I appreciate your cooking. You wouldn't want to slave over a hot stove for nothing, would you?'

'I have better things to do with my time. Like strangling you with this tea towel.'

Nell ran out of the kitchen with the tea-pot. Bea poked the bubbling pot of gooseberries; she had lost account of the time they had been cooking. It was true, after all, she did have better things to do with her time. She had to stay around, it didn't matter that Nell and Ginny might not really notice her absence. Nothing was going to get her for a few years yet. She set the second batch of gooseberries to cool. Nell had put the tea-pot on the draining board.

'You'd better pour a cup for granny. She'll be sitting on the lawn.'

Nell shook her head, banging the kettle down onto the stove: 'I'll pour and you can take it. I'll put a slice of cake on the tray as well.'

Bea looked over from the mounds of steaming fruit in the sink; Nell was arranging cup and saucer, a tiny sliver of cake on a tray.

'Why don't you want to take it, Nell?'

'I just don't feel like it.' She poured herself a mug of tea, 'I'm going to eat my tea in the garden,' and she had gone, carrying the mug and a wedge of cake.

Bea turned off the heat under the gooseberries and poured tea into the thin cup Nell had set out. She took the tray outside, along the stone paths to the edge of the lawn. The chair was set under the apple tree in the corner, turned away from her; in the shade she glimpsed the vague outline of a book tossed onto the grass, a square of print dress. Bea walked silently across the shimmering lawn. The distance seemed immense. She could see the pale fragile hands clasped loosely in the lap, the head resting gently against the back of the deckchair. She brings elegance to this life of immobility, Bea thought, she almost gives it point. As if it were an art, to live out one's old age in tranquillity in the shade of the trees. She looked down at the tray — Nell's acknowledgement of what her grandmother lived by.

Bea stood by the chair: 'I've brought you a little tea, Ada.'

'Oh, there you are, Beatrice. I have been sitting here so pleasantly under the trees.'

'Perhaps we could have dinner outside this evening.' Bea sat down on the grass with her back against the tree.

Ada sipped at her tea, 'It is certainly very warm still. I shouldn't like to be in the city in this weather.'

'I expect they have fans and things.' Bea contemplated the mounds of fruit in the kitchen; they would have to have some of it raw for supper.

'And where is Nell?'

'In the garden somewhere. Probably back in the fruit-cage.'

'I haven't seen her all afternoon.'

'She set your tea-tray. I think she's taken up with some new scheme about how the fruit should be picked more scientifically.' How neatly, Bea thought, the generations spread out in circles, Nell crouched in the red currants scheming to change the world. I turning in circles in the kitchen, hands to the stove, to the children, to Tim's three courses. And Ada sits still as ice in this chair, willing herself to withdraw from the world outside. Willing herself to do what she has to do. No wonder Nell wants nothing to do with either of us — it would be like seeing a speeded-up film — childhood — motherhood — old age — with the bits in between reduced to a blur of featureless tape, a few flickering seconds.

'Have you been picking fruit all this time? You look tired. You don't have to go at it in a rush like that, you know.'

Bea opened her eyes, 'I'm not really tired, Ada.' She looked up through the branches above her. The apples were ripening fast. 'Or perhaps it's being in touch with the seasons that's wearing. Makes one feel one's age.'

'I wouldn't have thought of you as an elemental figure, dear.' Ada eased herself carefully out of the chair, 'Perhaps I should come and give you a hand with the fruit. I find that summer is very good for the bones. Makes me feel quite ten years younger.'

* * * * * * * * * * * * * * *

Dee cut a slice of bread and submerged it in the juice on her plate. 'Ok, so I shouldn't have withdrawn like that. But I thought I was having to carry it all — and you two could bicker and I would have to lay soothing hands all over the place.'

'You created the situation in the first place.' Ann reached the tobacco from her pocket.

'It was you that insisted on coming over —'

Ann lit her cigarette and tossed the spent match towards the sink. 'And I was supposed to sit under a rock and remain invisible while you and Eleanor reached agreements about how undesirable I am? Look, Dee, I expect a little more support —'

Dee pushed back her chair, 'You didn't have to come charging in lit up like the avenging angel.'

'You're getting your metaphors mixed.'

'I expect so, you know damn well what I mean. When you walk in claiming to be the best thing since sliced bread my sympathies tend to go with whoever it is whose way of life you're currently spitting on.'

Ann stood by the window. Her hands were shaking; she folded them into her armpits. 'I believe in what I'm doing,' she said.

'I know you do. So do I —' Dee shrugged, spreading her arms to Ann's back turned at the window. She drew a cigarette out of her pocket and looked at it, 'It's not your being convinced that I'm complaining about, of course it isn't.' Dee paused, thinking of the two of them, Eleanor grinning, Ann lifting her eyebrows. 'The point is that you think that if she doesn't agree with you she has nothing but contempt for your views. And so you try to leap in first and set up your own scorn as a barrier.'

'I suppose that's true.' Ann huddled into herself a little more; it sounded familiar at any rate. She shouldn't have taken Eleanor so seriously. She picked up the half-smoked cigarette from the draining board, relit it. But Dee, surely she should take Dee seriously.

'I can see why you might decide you'd had enough — I mean I can see why you started eating biscuits.' She turned round — but her hand still shook. She turned back to the window. She went on, 'But I don't see why you brought up exhibiting at the W.I. Or at least I think that perhaps I do, and don't like it. It seemed to me that you were waiting for me to make

81

snide remarks about the W.I. and have Eleanor shred me for doing so. I felt that you were abandoning me for Eleanor.'

Ann poked the butt of the cigarette down the drain. She listened to the silence, to Dee not breaking the silence. As true as that then. Undeniable. I am surprised, I am relieved, she thought dully, holding herself still. I must not react yet, let the silence lengthen.

Dee fiddled with the bread knife, running her finger along its blunt little teeth. Just for a moment, she thought, I always want to let it go. Let it run. The effort of denial seems enormous. It even seems impossible, as if Ann is unshakeable. As if she has found something she wants to believe. But this is nothing, really. I only have to say that. She put down the knife, 'Of course I wasn't setting you up. There was a minimal abandonment – if you want to call it that – to the extent that I thought you were exaggerating the artistic isolation. I am certainly not abandoning you for Eleanor. You're letting language run away with you.' Dee picked up the cigarette she had discarded at the side of her plate, 'If I can't disagree with you and agree with Eleanor without being suspected of infidelity –'

Ann turned round, 'Of course it sounds ridiculous. It's the question of intention that matters. And whether my work can mean anything to the rest of the world is quite a significant question as far as I'm concerned.'

Dee stood up. She unfolded Ann's arms and took hold of her hands, 'I know that. And you know I think it can. If I thought it was impossible for us to speak to anyone else, how could I justify living like this? But I also don't see why you don't try exhibiting in places like the W.I., because it is accessible. Because we're not so different from them.'

Ann shook her head, 'They'll think my vision is tainted, like Eleanor does.'

Dee gathered her hands around Ann's back, spreading her fingers among the thin bones. 'It's not you that you're trying to sell them, is it? You're trying to present insights which have to do with their own situation in the world. Things we have in common.' Dee laid her cheek along Ann's shoulder, 'Oh, you know what I'm trying to say, don't you?' Ann's skin smelt of outdoors, as if she had brought the rain in with her.

Ann laughed, running her hands over the solidity of Dee's flesh, 'I know, telling them what they know already.' She stood close, wrapping herself in the heat of Dee's body. 'They're very resistant' she murmured, 'to the idea that women are wonderful. Much easier to agree that their husbands are intolerable.' She held her hands under the warmth of Dee's jersey, 'Then they say they have to put up with it.'

'Well, they do, don't they. There's no choice for almost all of them.'

Ann huddled. 'But I don't want them to have to put up with it. I don't want them to.' She cried, tears falling on Dee's neck. Dee stood silent, her hands laced into Ann's hair, feeling herself absorbed into Ann's anger through her own damp skin, the wetness seeping down her breast bone.

Ann sniffed. She laughed, her body shaking in Dee's arms. 'I can hardly put up with you,' she gasped, 'how can they bear so much more?'

Dee stepped back, jolted. 'Oh, it comes to much the same,' she said, 'women are just as unpleasant as men when it comes to living with them.'

Ann stared at her over her handkerchief, 'What is the matter, Dee? Of course they're not. You know you couldn't — that power, the power the world gives them hanging over you all the time? Reinforcing the status quo?'

Dee sat on the edge of the table, shaking her head. 'I don't know.' She covered her face with her hands.

'What is it, tell me, for god's sake!'

'It's very silly —' Dee accepted the handkerchief, 'only that I was a mass of sympathy for what you were saying, about how unbearable the world is — and then you said you could hardly put up with me.' She stuttered, waving her arms, 'Of course, I know what you mean, you're insufferable, I'm insufferable, the world —'

Ann picked up the cigarette from the table, put it down again. They were both silent for a moment. 'It's been a terrible day,' Ann said, 'can't we cheer ourselves up somehow?'

'It's raining again. I'd say it was a choice between schools programmes on the telly or going to bed.'

'I'd quite like to go to bed if that suits you.' She picked up the cigarette again, 'But you'll have to take that woman's sweater off.'

Not chaos but dissolution. Neither in either but towards each. How I struggle to define. Dee reached out her hand for Ann's hair: I ground myself. The hair under my fingers, hers. The blood rushing along my legs, inhabiting my toes, mine. We have called this up. Behind my eyes, colours: earthenware, terracotta. She asks I obliterate boundaries, I do not want them. We are attending to each other, so carefully. I trust, she wants all this. Here it is. Dee felt Ann's body reemerge above her and settle its limbs about her. She clung to it, her eyes snapped open. A new definition of chaos, she thought.

* * * * * * * * * * * * * * *

Eleanor turned out of the village high street. The roar of the juke-box swelled from the open door of the pub and walked with her far down the lane. But there was no one about, the light slanting across empty fields. It will be dark on the way back, she thought, I should have brought a torch. But I haven't a torch. All these years living here I've never needed one. They ferry you to and fro for their little parties, don't they, as if there were still only the one car to the village. I hadn't thought to go to this one. Their pictures, their casual invitations. Just another rat to put through the maze. What will it do, faced with these pictures? But then, Dee squatting on a sack of potatoes, offering days of the week. Leaning in the doorway, conjuring her new recipe in the air. Ann dropping in to lay her smile here and there about the shop. It was flattering to be so bothered with. They'd gone all out for her. These advances, though, she could've turned them off, and hadn't. She bent down and deposited her two parcels in the grass. The bag she had wrapped over the pineapple was splitting, fragments of brown paper adhering to the bulbous spines. She removed the bag and crumpled it into her pocket. There was no hiding it, after all. Sitting lopsided in the grass, dingy in the dying light, it did not look, Eleanor thought, like the right sort of thing to bring when asked out to dinner. What would they want with it? Ugly thing, only fit for children's parties. Something someone might bring back from overseas. Can't leave it here by the side of the road. Eleanor lifted the pineapple into the crook of her arm and grasped the bottle of wine in her other hand. That was what you did, surely, bring bottles of wine? Or it was what they did, to each other — they would know it was nothing to do with what she thought the done thing. I feel older the nearer I get, she thought.

I could not have come. But not without losing it, losing the link. Denying what was once. I don't seem to want to do that, cut myself off. Not any more, though I had, was a long way away from all that. But these two, only being here, make me twitch, itch, move as if there were something burrowing into me. Make me move at random, as if I'd lost my bearings. It doesn't make sense, to move towards them, just because they've become some sort of — catalyst. Eleanor paused at the gate. Knowing them, I shall know where I am. She lifted the latch and walked quietly up the path.

Ann opened the door, 'I saw you coming.'

'I have this pineapple.' Eleanor thrust her burdens across the threshold, 'I'm sure it was the wrong thing to bring.'

Ann weighed it in her hands, 'It looks very luxurious, exotic. An entirely appropriate gift from a fruiterer. I shall enshrine it in the fruit bowl.' She bore it off into the living room.

Eleanor followed her, 'I deserve teasing for it, no doubt. It's the kind of thing grandmothers might give to save your teeth. I would have a handful of mixed nuts in my pocket to give out when the kids got too boisterous.'

Ann laughed, pointing Eleanor in the direction of the fire. 'Dee's cycled off for some wine — she'll be back in a minute. Do you attend gatherings like that?'

Eleanor shook her head, 'No, no, I must be thinking of some traditional version of family life — got it from the pictures, probably. The odd grandparent I remember was glad enough to get its teeth into whatever there was about.' She watched Ann, perched on the arm of a chair, rolling a cigarette. 'And no grandchildren, of course,' she added. Of course. They could tell that from — what exactly? No signs were so conclusive, were they? the business, the living alone? That could mean divorce, death, the children gone. No — Eleanor leaned back into a corner of the settee — there was no getting round it. She was just what they expected, a thin shrivelled taciturn spinster. She laughed suddenly, feeling in her pockets for cigarettes.

'What is it?' Ann inquired, reaching up to the mantelpiece for an ash-tray.

'It occurred to me that they don't run glamorous spinster competitions for the over-fifties who aren't grandmothers.'

'Or for various other categories of non-woman. And the only other competition available is champion homemaker. With no prizes.'

Eleanor only searched for cigarettes.

'Damn' she said, after a while.

'Have you left your cigarettes behind? Shall I roll you one of these?'

Eleanor glanced over; Ann balanced, materials spread on her knee. Does she really think I want such things, a place in beauty competitions? Must only want to dissect me like a rat, then. My little secret about Bea that I'm hoarding for them. Thought I would tell them tonight. Thought it would make them see me differently, somehow. Probably still seem an untutored old woman. I don't know why I go on.

'I'd like to try one of those.'

Ann nodded and Eleanor watched as the thin white cylinder appeared beneath Ann's fingers. The cigarette passed between them. I only roll for my friends, Ann found herself thinking as Eleanor leaned away. Old rituals go on. The exchange of food appeases.

'There are other competitions.'

But Ann listening heard the lightness of tone. The charm holds, she thought. She shrugged, 'For women? There are men's competitions, of course. In which the odds are set against us, and where we are always supposed not really to be entered at all. You run a shop, for instance; and yet you are forced to be aware that you've failed because you're not eligible for beauty contests. A business man succeeds as a man by virtue of his business.'

'Not much of a yardstick.'

'No — but no more are beauty contests. I'm only talking about what is, and not what ought.'

Eleanor blew smoke towards the ceiling, 'And what ought?'

Ann tipped herself into the depths of her armchair, 'Oh, not yet, please —'

The two women grinned at each other across the purple rug. 'We could make a start on the wine I brought. That might encourage you,' Eleanor said, 'or does wine make you quarrelsome?'

Ann grinned again: 'Perhaps I should roll a store of cigarettes for when we both get drunk.'

They both turned at a noise from the kitchen. 'It's Dee,' Ann said, 'now we can all three drink.'

Dee smiled, swirling a little wine at the bottom of her glass. On either side of her Ann and Eleanor smoked in silence, loose in their chairs. She swirled the wine gently, not to disturb their slow, peaceful movements, the even spiral of the smoke. Like lizards, she thought, slowed by the sun, basking. This moment of comfort, let it be elongated, so that we can feel it actual between us, something that has significance.

Ann turned her head, smiled. After a moment she said: 'I could make it a series, "woman with a wine-glass".'

Eleanor turned, that same slow movement of the head, and looked at Dee. They feel it, Dee realised, they feel it too — we are all catching hold of it, playing with it, embroidering it.

'You mean,' said Eleanor, 'you have a series of pictures of Dee?'

Ann watched the colour in Dee's cheeks, the colour brought by the wine; the tension between that, and her look of absorption, of her thoughts ranging away from the glass. It would be, if she had after all been Rembrandt, an erotic picture. About how she was always, there and not there. Hot limbs and her thoughts anywhere. How I want sometimes to bring them to the same certainty, my simplicity. Those easy guttural colours that she hands me and I sink into so readily, mind knees-wide. And Dee, darling Dee, takes my simple sensations and climbs ladders with her hand in my hair.

'Oh yes,' she said, 'I'm always drawing Dee. I just like to, I like the way she looks, that's all. Mostly just messages passed between us.'

'It sounds,' Eleanor paused, wondering. It sounded idyllic —intelligent gestures of attention and affection. Did it? Or was there a great flow of sentiment that the wine had unleashed in her brain washing over this, making what was only excessive, charming? 'It sounds' she said at last, 'better than any messages I ever passed.'

Dee raised her head: 'What were your messages?'

Eleanor searched for phrases; direct ones eluded her. She saw herself drawing out a hopeless vague string of talk: messages, gifts, secrets. And the simple story left unsaid. 'There was a woman,' she said. Dee had filled her glass. 'I used to write her messages.' Eleanor picked up the wine that Dee had pushed towards her. 'They used to say things like —' It was impossible. She could not.

Ann was rolling cigarettes, had reached across the table and placed one by her hand. She picked it up. 'Oh god. They used to say things like, I love you how about lunch today.' Dee was holding out a match. Eleanor lit the cigarette and laughed, waving smoke away, 'I used to slip them into files of correspondence. I was twenty-five and curiously innocent. Her name was Beatrice Carmichael and she was what was known as a cut above me. Several, in fact.'

Eleanor felt herself launched on an irresistible tide of reminiscence. She hardly hesitated, reaching out to those strange, distant details that suddenly floated in front of her, each separate, brightly-lit. 'I took up the violin in London and met her at the firm's orchestra. You went there for the young men, they had wet lips and played wind instruments. I was in the depths of the second violins and Bea played in the firsts, they all went for her, of course. We used to go out together in foursomes —' Eleanor stopped. 'This must all seem very distant to you.'

Ann shook her head, 'It's just the same, nothing's changed.' They really were there, she thought gladly. All over the place. Just outside your range of vision, only waiting to be seen. That was how it should be. No need to feel this great leap of surprise.

'I did that too,' Dee said, 'except I never managed the transition between going out in foursomes with them and in a twosome with her. I wouldn't have known how to do that.' She managed, Dee thought. I thought it wasn't possible. Because I didn't. Eleanor is stronger than me.

'We went on holiday together. I think we meant to carry on with our foursomes by the seaside, but we – well.' Eleanor looked over Ann's head to the yellowing plaster of the wall. It was spread with faint stains as if someone long since had thrown tea. 'Found an opportunity. Fell into each other's arms.'

'How very romantic.' Ann reached for the fruit bowl. She began to score lines through the peel of an orange. How neat, she thought, how much more as things should be. Falling into each other's arms with a gasp of passion. So much easier to justify being a lesbian when you fall into the arms of the love of your life without pain. She peeled off the skin of the orange in segments; none of that vague undirected groping. Those spasms of self-disgust. The orange split into two halves. 'Didn't you worry about what you were doing?' she asked. 'That it was wrong?'

Eleanor saw Bea lifting her arm from between the sheets and turning it in the candlelight, hand raised towards the ceiling; the two of them watching her slow movements in a glaze of contentment. They had hardly thought at all, beyond the confines of each other. 'Not at first,' she said, 'we were so absorbed, as if we had uncovered a secret.' She stubbed out her cigarette abruptly, 'We were very naive.' She looked down at her plate, 'It was a long time ago.'

Dee shifted forward in her chair and picked up the wine bottle. She measured what remained into their three glasses. 'But what happened?' she said.

Eleanor sat staring in front of her; Ann's hands were gathered inert around the orange dissected on her plate.

'What usually happens,' Ann said bitterly, 'is that they go off and marry someone. And you feel a right fool.'

Dee reached for her hand across the table. 'It isn't always like that, not this universal betrayal. Women are always leaving their husbands and their lovers.'

'And then they go back to them.'

'What about all the ones who don't, who stagger on –'

'Do they?' Eleanor asked.

Dee looked from one to the other – what did they want, that the world should change overnight? Medals for endurance? 'Of course they do. There must be hundreds dug in all over the place –'

Eleanor laughed, lifting her glass, 'Like the home guard.' She turned to Dee, 'Perhaps it's easier if you think there's a war on, that you're fighting for something.' She shrugged: 'When you just think you're going out on a limb because you want something different and no one else approves – you tend to think you're misguided.' Her voice fell away.

'But there is a war on.' Dee leaned forward. She still grasped Ann's hand. These two women seem to act upon me when we're together, she thought, I feel like an insane optimist. And I want to hold Eleanor's hand too. As if these simple comforts will make her believe in the goodness of humanity, or something. Eleanor was staring into the distance. It seemed to Dee, watching her, that the lines networking her face had become more apparent, as though it were attention, consciousness, that held them at bay. But perhaps she isn't trying to hold them off, why should she want to hang on to her youth. They are there. Sometimes I notice them.

'Did Beatrice marry someone?' she asked.

Eleanor smiled faintly, raising her head, 'Yes, she did,' she said finally.

'Oh dear.' Ann picked at the segments of orange.

'I didn't really try to intervene, though.' Eleanor spoke slowly, running her finger along the waxed table top. Her voice was vague, unsteady, almost puzzled, 'And I could have, I could have. It seemed in some ways inevitable, d'you see? The way things were. How could I hold Bea away from that? Her position in life.'

Ann looked over at Dee, at their hands clasped, parading ease. 'She wanted that position?' And that was a stupid question, Ann thought, don't we all. She took her hand from Dee's and began to roll cigarettes.

'I think,' Eleanor gathered herself. She would round it off, finish it. Set it out and have done with it. Better to have it over and out of the way and not sit here any longer, draining scenes from endless memory. 'I think that she wanted very much to be reassured that some other way of life was possible. But I wasn't prepared to do much pleading – I wanted her to be convinced. Not to have to beg. I didn't want to beg off the rich.' Ann pushed a cigarette over, handed one to Dee. Eleanor drove on: 'And then I justified it. It wouldn't've lasted. We would've blamed each other. It wouldn't've been any different from anything else and so not worth all the difficulties. And so on.' She looked up from the table to Ann and Dee's stares. 'Does it seem so strange?' She spread her hands: 'It did seem to leave me not wanting to do that — get involved — again.'

'It seems unbearable,' Ann said quietly.

'Unbearable? All those things are true — it wouldn't've lasted.'

'But you would have had it,' Dee said suddenly, forcefully. 'It wouldn't be making you nearly as miserable now as it is if you'd at least tried. There is something in it, you know — that's the whole point, isn't it, that for all its imperfections and the nasty things that happen because we believe people when they say it's wrong and evil and perverted — the point is that it's better than what else there is — that loving women are good for each other?' Dee stood up and began to stride up and down the room. 'I'm sorry if I'm being stupid and simplistic and naive. But you're sitting there talking as if the mark of Cain was on lesbians and Ann is acting as if it's all hopeless for the next thousand years.' Dee came to a stop in the doorway: 'I'll put a kettle on. I can't bear this. I'll take my rude hope and belief in women elsewhere.'

Eleanor settled back into the corner of the settee and warmed her hands around her mug. 'I can see that you might be right in general,' she said, 'I find it difficult to apply to myself, though.' She held herself carefully, wary of stray thoughts. I am too tired, I am worn down, she thought. I cannot tolerate any more. They've given me the sleep deprivation and the interrogator has offered me cigarettes.

Ann stood up from the rug: 'I'm going to fetch something.'

Dee listened to the footsteps overhead. Time to abandon the argument. She had only wanted to be helpful; but it looked as if Eleanor did not want to think that Beatrice might still be within reach. Dee glanced up from the floor at her: she had been clumsy, horribly clumsy.

Eleanor sat with her eyes almost closed. Ann's footsteps clattered down the stairs and she came in carrying a little statue, the woman she had done for Amy years before. She put it on the arm of the settee. 'There you are — crude belief in women! I did it a while ago — it really is a bit crude, one of my first efforts.'

Eleanor reached out gingerly and touched it. She liked it, she could see that it could be stirring, stirring them on to battle. But at what a distance from her, her present. She let her hand fall back to her lap. She looked from Ann to Dee. 'May I look at it again some other time? I don't feel as if I can take it in just now.'

Ann put the statue on the mantelpiece. Have we really been at her so much, she wondered? She stood still, not knowing what she could say that would not seem like another assault. 'We could eat the pineapple,' she said bleakly.

Eleanor smiled: 'I could manage that.'

* * * * * * * * * * * * * * *

Bea stood at Nell's bedroom window watching a rotting elm swaying in the wind. She often came up here to watch it, resting the palms of her hands along the clean white paint of the window sill. Trying to calculate where it might fall if it fell towards the house. Today the wind gusted, rocking the tree and forcing its way under the window to stir the curtains. There had once been a line of elms, large and alive and green, where that rotting hulk stood. The view from Nell's window had changed with their felling: now you could see further, across more flat fenced and hedgeless fields. Bea lifted her hands from the cold sill and flicked dust from the corners of the window panes. She turned away from the window. All round the room the shelves were empty, bare glass, bare paint. The dahlias she had put on the bedside table, rich dark red in the garden, looked greyish in the dim afternoon light.

So Nell was coming to stay for a few days. To stay here in this cold hotel room. Bea crossed to the wardrobe and drew back the doors. There was a jangle of coat hangers. She looked inside: an old coat swung there. Bea looked at it, she did not recognise it. Finally she put out a hand and lifted the cloth between her fingers. A tartan lining — perhaps it was only an old school coat — there had been so many. She shut the doors again quickly, and the coat hangers jangled.

When she stepped out of the house the wind swept through her jersey and she hurried along the path. At the door to Tim's shed a rambling rose had left drifts of shrivelling pink petals against the steps. She scrunched through them and went in. Inside Tim sat hunched over a piece of paper. Bea hung back for a moment; then she crossed to a shelf piled with seed packets and began to shuffle through them. 'What are you doing?' she asked.

'Trying to work out how the vegetables should be rotated for next year.' Tim spread two pieces of paper out next to each other and looked from one to the other, 'I hate doing this — always seem to be too many things to fit in somewhere.'

Bea put a wadge of packets back on the shelf, 'Why don't you grow less?'

Tim considered. 'Could do, of course. Maybe I will. But one doesn't know where to start, does one?'

Bea turned from the seeds: 'No. I see that. All or nothing.' She ran her hand slowly along the shelf, picked up a ball of string. 'You remember Nell is coming?'

Tim looked up: 'Yes, is she coming soon? Is it for long?'

'Only the week-end. She'll be here this evening.'

Bea wound string tightly round her finger. 'I don't know why she's coming,' she said.

'What do you mean?'

Bea unwrapped the string. Her finger had reddened. She bound a second finger more tightly, in layer after layer of string. 'If I were her,' she said, 'I wouldn't come here.' Her finger throbbed through the string.

'She knows we like to see her. Of course,' he said, folding the vegetable diagram neatly, 'she has her own life, but the occasional visit, it's not too much to ask —'

Bea gestured impatiently: 'I think it's a great deal. It's like a mausoleum here. Have you tried walking into either of the girls' rooms lately? They're like uninhabited hotels, cardboard sets, institutions.' She shrugged: 'Uninhabited.' She let her hands fall loose; the string spilled slowly away from her aching finger.

Tim doodled on the pad in front of him. 'I know it's hard,' he said quietly, 'I know it's hard to accept that our function is over, that they don't need us any more, but it's inevitable, Bea, you know that. I know it's hard for you especially.'

Bea shook her head, 'It's not that, Tim. No,' she put the string back on the shelf, 'it's the quality of what's left that I can't stand, as if that awful greyness were starting in their rooms and radiating through the house —' she stood by his stool, reached out a hand to straighten the heap of pencils on the table, 'it reaches me, Tim, it inhabits me. Like a disease, like dying on your feet. I don't just feel purposeless, do you understand? I feel like an empty shell.'

Tim drew lines on the pad and then laid down his pencil. 'But you're saying just what I meant — of course you feel purposeless and empty, without the children to occupy you. It's natural —'

Bea put her head suddenly in her hands, 'No! No, no, I'll not find things to do with my time. I won't. If I stay in this house like this I'll become — I'll become like your mother.'

Tim sat in silence, stunned. 'I think my mother had a very happy old age,' he said at last.

Bea lifted her head, 'She did it beautifully, I always thought so. Right to the very end she played the perfect grandmother. Never betrayed the family honour by one sign of discontent with her miserable lot.'

'Her miserable lot?' He stared at her in surprise.

Bea stood silent for a moment, meeting his look. 'Her complete irrelevance,' she said.

Tim smiled, 'We can't all be Chairman Mao.' He gestured: 'I suppose I shall be pretty irrelevant too, when I get to be eighty.' He was not quite able to imagine it. But there was no need to anticipate.

Bea laid her hand on his arm, feeling the soft expensive wool beneath her fingers, 'But that's it,' she said insistently, 'you won't want to feel irrelevant then any more than you do now. One has to hold it off as long as possible. Make oneself feel relevant — somehow. I can't resign myself to becoming a grandmother for the next thirty years.'

'I suppose not,' Tim sounded confused. 'Shall we go in and have a drink to aid the thought processes?'

Bea loosened her hold. 'All right,' she said, following Tim out of the shed. The wind flung the door to behind her.

Tim paused in the path: 'What an autumnal wind!' he called over his shoulder.

Bea turned the phrase in her mind as she wrapped her arms about her and hurried across to the house. The autumn of my fiftieth year began early, that had a fine epic quality to it, she thought. But autumn? This was just a passing wind. And she was not yet fifty.

'I don't really know what it is you want,' Tim said, refilling her glass.

'Nor do I.' Bea whirled the stem of her glass between her fingers.

'You could always go back to work, I suppose.'

'What as?'

'You used to work in an office, didn't you?'

Bea drained her glass: 'That was before the children were born, Tim.'

'Well, but you could go back to it — there's a market these days for mature reliable secretaries.' Tim warmed to the idea as he spoke. They would have to eat more out of the freezer of course, that kind of thing, make the domestic arrangements tighter. But it would certainly be good for Bea to keep busy, see the world a little. 'I think it's an excellent idea,' he pronounced, pacing backwards and forwards across the carpet, 'of course we'd have to reorganise ourselves a little, but there's no harm in that.'

'I don't really see the point of passing the time just for the sake of it.' Bea watched him halt at the fireplace, set his glass carefully down on the mantel.

'Well, if that's really so, dear, there's only religion left you, isn't there?'

Or an affair, Bea thought, that's another traditional refuge. But if I mention it he might think I meant it. It does seem more likely. More of the same. I shall try not to fall for that. She got up, 'I suppose you're right, it would be better to have something to do.'

'Why don't you come up to town with me on Monday, then, and go round a few agencies, see how the land lies?'

Bea nodded: 'All right – I may as well make a move, mayn't I.' She looked over at him. She had gone to him for help, after all. Perhaps this was what she had been wanting.

Bea watched the back of Tim's head disappearing down the steps into the underground. She joined a second rush of suited people striding towards the Bakerloo line. On the platform she checked her list of addresses; it would be best to start from a point where a number of these places were within walking distance. May as well approach it methodically. She moved forward as a train arrived; amongst those suits pushing their way in, her coloured outfit looked frivolous. A shopper who had mistaken her route to the department stores and intruded on the calm seriousness of working lives. Where are the office girls, she wondered, looking up and down the carriage, what about all those I used to travel with, the secretaries? They can't have disappeared, she thought – it's as if they've been blotted out. The idea was disturbing, as if in a dream she had got into the wrong carriage and been swept away in the company of grey-suited aliens. A man beside her looked at his watch. That was the answer, of course, the time. The office girls would have been at work for over an hour. These all around her were the strange exotic men, senior partners or directors perhaps, whose hours were not vulgarly prescribed. Who might arrive at the office for an hour or two before lunch. Bea looked around her again; I still hate them, she thought with surprise, just like I used to, meeting them on the way to work after the dentist. How ridiculous, when I've been having them to dinner for all these years. I even live with one. But she found herself scowling still as she left them and turned to find her way to the first agency on her list.

You're out of touch, Beatrice, she thought as she watched the woman across the desk draw a form towards her. Sharp angles, navy suit, the scarf tied at the neck, everything matches. She had forgotten, it seemed, quite what city elegance required.

'Do smoke if you want to,' the woman smiled graciously, 'and when was it that you last worked?'

'Before my children were born.'

The woman smiled slightly, 'And when was that, exactly?'

I should have thought out my tactics, Bea thought. '1956,' she said.

'And you haven't worked at all since then?'

'Well, no — they were a full-time occupation, what with the house to —'

'I quite understand,' she broke in soothingly, 'we get quite a few ex-mothers, so to speak, coming to us.'

She filled in boxes on the form in front of her. Bea contemplated the tip of her cigarette: ex-mother.

'I expect your skills are rather rusty?'

'Skills?' Bea looked at her blankly for a moment. 'Oh, yes — well, I don't think one forgets these things, do you?'

The woman eyed her, her biro poised: 'But you haven't made any special effort to keep your hand in.'

'A couple of hours of shorthand nightly before retiring?' Bea shook her head, 'I'm afraid I never thought of it.'

'Why should you, indeed?' The biro descended. 'I don't think we can ask the very highest salary, do you? Lacking a bit of polish after all these years — shall we say two and a half to three thousand?'

Bea remembered the advertisements in the window. 'That's rather less than you're offering temporary typists,' she observed, flicking ash lightly from her cigarette.

The woman leaned back in her chair, 'Temps have no security, you know, Mrs Lloyd — and that's worth a good deal.' She smiled, a momentary smile of complicity, 'And temping's very much a young girl's game, I'm afraid.'

'I do have other qualifications, of a more general nature, office manager, that kind of thing.'

She was brusque, 'No use at all, I'm afraid, Mrs Lloyd — those are career skills, a quite different market. You wouldn't have much hope of getting in there.'

Bea smiled resolutely: 'Then you must just put three to three and a half thousand. I wouldn't want them to think I'm desperate.'

On the pavement Bea consulted her list. There was a cafe across the road. Inside she stared down at the plastic dishes filled with anchovies and cheese and salad and salami. She had forgotten the sandwiches. Sandwiches and frothy coffee for lunch.

'I'll have a cream cheese and anchovy and a beef with onion. On brown. And a coffee,' she said, simply for the pleasure of remembering the code, the right combinations.

'Right you are, anchovy,' he said, reaching into the cabinet.

She sat down at a table and took an old envelope out of her bag. She would have to go about this differently. A list of qualifications, perhaps. 'Proven organisational' she wrote. As evidenced in running of large house in commuter heartland. She wrote a few more lines, looked back at what she had written. I really can't take this seriously, she thought. I don't even want to be somebody's secretary, doing all those housewively things I have been doing already. She bit into the tart anchovy sandwich. Well, why work, after all? Just come up to London suitably dressed, to go to a museum perhaps, eavesdrop on a few conversations. And eat lunch in a different sandwich bar every day. Return home on a suitable train in time to pick up the threads of the day, hoover the carpet, put together a little supper. Bea lifted a corner of her beef sandwich; it looked overdone. She could tell herself she was researching a guide to the sandwich bars of London: what every office girl needs in her handbag. The truth about the ones near you. The ones worth an expedition. Ringing the changes: the author's menu suggestions for jaded palates. Luncheon vouchers and your diet. Bea thrust her sandwich ends to the side of the plate; this was no good. Decision making: the next agency. Selling herself. But she could not bring her mind round to that just yet.

I can just see myself, wandering around London day after day, correctly dressed. By myself, listening to other people. Eating in sandwich bars. The plausibility of it frightened her. If I could think of something I wanted. She stood up and carried her cup to the counter for more coffee. Are sandwich lunches a sufficient reason for living. That's the worst of it, she thought, settling herself again, even I can't take my discontent seriously. She reread the list on the envelope. Why should they welcome me like a prodigal daughter, after all. There they've been grinding away all this time and I waltz in demanding a job after twenty-five years of being somebody's wife. Being kept in silk scarves. What was it Tim had been saying on the train: 'I expect it'll be worth our while to be taxed separately.' My very own silk scarves. Economic independence, said to do wonders for the redundant mother's self-respect. Or call it pin-money, depends on your point of view. Because, Bea thought, I don't know whether I could live on two and a half thousand a year. Not with scarves, at any rate. Add to the sandwich bar guide: lunching on two thousand a year. And. Sandwiches you can make yourself. Hints from the austere fifties on how to make the most of a stale loaf of bread. I wonder how much Eleanor is living on these days. Let it be more than two and a half thousand a year. Bea considered the odd card she had had; not the very cheapest kind – but then that might be deliberate concealment. She might have been starving all along and not have wanted me to know. And I never even considered it. But the shop, she remembered, the shop. That surely must make her a decent living.

Bea was on a bus travelling up the Marylebone Road. She had been to all the agencies on her list. We'll be in touch. Tuesday afternoon, a day and a half. You will be available won't you Mrs Lloyd. Don't leave the 'phone unattended, will you. Things can come up at such short notice.

The bus stopped, wedged tight in the traffic. Bea got off. Here I go, she thought, my random wandering begins. She looked about her – Regent's Park wouldn't be far away – she made towards it with relief. Visiting the rose garden sounded quite sensible. So long as she kept away from the zoo. Desperate old women muttering to the monkeys, jamming guilty peanuts through the bars.

The roses seemed tired. The climbers sagged on their trellises, as if the season had been too long, the strain of daily performances terrible. Bea found a bench elsewhere, beside a patch of grass, a place empty of the struggle to keep up appearances. But there's nothing to look at, Bea realised when she had eased her shoes from her feet, only the people passing. That was what one did, of course: sit and watch the world go by. Bea searched through her bag for cigarettes. Here we are again, then. Perhaps Ada had been right after all; she certainly had more dignity. Had even managed to die with dignity. Without hospital lights or surgical explorations. Only a last cup of morning tea forming a skin by the bedside. But then, she'd had twenty years to prepare for it. Concentrate on making a decent death. Perhaps that was the only choice — dignity or the lack of it. Bea blew smoke into the air; whether to sit on a bench in the park calling derisively to the couples on the grass, you'll come to this, all to this. Or to fold one's hands in one's lap in Camberley, thankful for the eggshell blue walls of one's granny flat around one.

I don't think I shall be able to do it, I haven't the courage, Bea thought. Tears came to her eyes; and she forced her attention away, to two figures wandering across the grass towards her, their arms around each other. As they came closer Bea realised that they were both women. She stared at them over her cigarette: they came on, heads together. Bea could hear them giggling composedly. One looked up, then, and registered her stare; she stared back as if she would pin Bea to the bench with her eyes. The other one glanced over, smiled slightly, and pivoted them both round. They set off again, ambling back the way they had come. Bea watched them out of sight. There was perhaps more to sitting on benches than met the eye, she told herself as they disappeared, she should stay and see what happened next. But she did not want to, after all. She wanted to move.

She gathered up her handbag and fitted herself back into her shoes. The path brought her out by a stretch of water and there she stopped again: there was no harm in looking at the ducks. For something about having seen those women troubled her; she felt guilty of something. What Tim, what most people would say went through her mind: in public; unnecessary; disgusting. If they must, not here. What would Ada have been able to say? Something about illness, perhaps. And she had only sat on a bench and stared. Well, what could she have done: shaken them by the hand, said I do understand? Did she understand? She could have done nothing. And yet, by sitting there, she had done something: she had become, for those two women, just what they would expect. A representative figure, the world in miniature propped up on a bench: come unto me and I shall disapprove, I am the unyielding tradition of centuries, carried on from hand to hand by those waiting to die. You shall all come to this, I'll see to that.

Bea's hand trembled as she took the cigarettes from her bag. She gripped her lighter tightly and stooped to set the bag carefully on the ground. I'll not take my place on that bench. A coot scuttled into the reeds at the other side of the water. Bea smoked steadily: the cigarette was calming. She finished it and ground the butt into the grass underfoot: I hardly know what I'm saying, she thought, it's this bench or nothing. And aren't I sitting on it already, lot cast with the scarf-wearers? They would say so, those two girls. My daughters would say so. My husband would say so. Ada and the other departed ghosts — they would say so. Bea picked up her bag and turned back towards the road. They would all say so.

Bea awoke to find Tim awake beside her. She turned her head, 'Can't you sleep?'

'You were snoring.'

'I'm sorry.'

'It's nearly time anyway — are you coming into town with me this morning?'

'Yes, I think so.' Better to keep moving. It was light, but early yet, the road outside still silent; at seven the first stream would be moving steadily past.

'I'll try not to snore any more,' she said, but Tim had drifted back into sleep. Bea lay on, her head turned to the window. She couldn't keep going up to London, pretending to look for a job. One of the agencies might find something — but not if they couldn't get her on the telephone. Because she was always in London. So she should stay here, sit in the sun with a good book, or shell peas. Just one more day. She would give herself one more day.

She went straight to the cafe at the station. The heart of London: you can get anywhere from here, once you have decided where you want to go. Bea arranged her coffee cup, her bag, to one side, her cigarettes and lighter in a little pile to the other. She opened the tube map: a wide range of choices. Any one of a number of parks — not parks, not benches, not people moving with sinister purposefulness across grass. That was the unnerving thing about parks, Bea thought, you never knew where anybody was going. Museums, tourist attractions, then. She considered: full of people outside themselves, playing at being on holiday, playing at being abnormal; how could I think amongst all those people behaving oddly? She could go out then, take a train far out until it stopped and wander there, where people lived. Muswell Hill. Stockwell. She could look in the newsagents' windows.

Bea leant back suddenly in her chair — surely that was not it. She had not found it. It was to be her last day and she didn't know what to do with it. Half-past ten already; in the offices the girls would be having coffee. Did they still, she wondered, hide packets of biscuits in their desks? And get hungry half-an-hour before lunch, and try to hide the scrunching under the shuffle of papers and the drum of your heels on the floor, so that they shouldn't catch you at it? Did they run offices like that still, like girls' schools, a mass of regulations and infringements and intrigue? And the men — things apart, whom you knew only by their handwriting and their occasional sudden intrusions, arriving only to speak to the office manager, always to complain. Eleanor coming in one morning, leaning over the desk. Flinging a biscuit down — stole it from a tray upstairs, going into conference it was, that biscuit! How absurd it had all been — playing like wayward children, playing to spite the ogre and not because you liked his garden so particularly. And yet Eleanor, bursting in with some scrap, something they weren't supposed to know, something they weren't supposed to eat — transformed into something worth having for its own sake. She used to carry these things in as if they were gifts, and the way she did it made them seem like it. I wonder if she still does that. I could go and find out.

For a moment she only sat still, staring into her empty cup. Then she gathered her things: she could just go and see if there was a train. She almost ran to the timetable, suddenly aware of the trains sliding away from the platforms every moment. There was a train; now she ran, guarding the impulse, to the ticket office, to the barrier, into a carriage.

Was she going to the right station? How would she get from there to the village? Supposing Eleanor were out, or had moved and not told her. As the train began its slow journey Bea leaned in a corner of the carriage and watched as from a distance these problems crowding the front of her mind. She was tired, as if the last few days had drained her of energy for considering the real questions, whatever they might turn out to be. And she found she was grateful for the respite. But as the train drew out into the country, past the reclaimed gravel pits, Bea sat up and reached for her handbag. She found Eleanor's address in the book — it wouldn't be so very far from the station. Why are you going, Beatrice, she asked herself then, drawing out a cigarette, don't you know there's no point?

She considered this, staring out of the window at shaved fields, fresh stubble spiny in the sun: Eleanor's attraction was of course that she was not Ada. She stood outside the line of succession. Or perhaps she did not

— perhaps there was another that Bea had not accounted for, the grave-yard of old spinster ladies? Or did she keep that at bay, because she worked, because she had always worked? Was she still grappling with two thousand a year? And so what, Bea thought wearily, if she is — it doesn't help me. She isn't going to help me; she isn't going to want to. What will she have to say to me after all these years, except — Bea laughed, picking a thread from her dark blue skirt — she did not even know how Eleanor would say it, say 'Go away'.

Perhaps it was dangerous to test that old image of Eleanor against the reality. Hadn't Eleanor become so much a symbol of other possibilities, those lives she had not led, that seeing her would only be useless? Wasn't the real Eleanor irrelevant? No doubt she had had some life, some different life. She would know about book-keeping, the wholesale price of plums. Perhaps she still played the violin in some orchestra. Went to dinner with the woodwind afterwards. What had that to do with what she had meant to me, with freedom and experience? How could anything she had done measure up to that — it could not, and it had not needed to. That had not been the point: Eleanor had stood out, out there, for what Bea herself didn't have; for clarity, when Nell and Ginny stood pressed thick around her, fleshy layers weighing her down, tearing her thoughts to frag-ments in her head. It had seemed to her then that Eleanor would have been able to think. And she had thought of her, alone and contemplative, a lone figure with its eyes pitched to the middle distance. What had this figure, this figure of speech, this abstraction, to do with Eleanor?

Bea leaned her arm along the window; outside a wood swept towards her, and then the line was running alongside a canal, had swung away again, was once more skirting a swell of stubble. Too fast, she thought, how it runs past me too fast. I want to grab at it, slow the train, meander through. Make it part of my time. However Eleanor was, it would prove nothing, she realised. Nothing about what she had lost or gained. What was she trying to do, after all, set up scales in which to weigh on the one side a fruit shop, on the other her children?

And now, she thought, I am taking myself off somewhere, to get away. She threw the stub down onto the floor of the carriage and drew out another cigarette. The lighter clicked in her hand and she bent her head towards the flame, precise, clothed in dark blue — aware at once of herself as elegant, perhaps alien, amidst the streaked drabness of the train, the cigarette ends underfoot. How easily she could get away: off at the next station, slipping her address book and cigarettes into her handbag. Take a turn about the town, see the church, find a quiet spot for lunch. And return home. A pleasant outing. So much more in keeping — for wasn't it a mistake, somehow, to take herself out of her own sphere? Ah, and there it was again. Her own sphere where Ada beckoned to a quiet place in the shade, where Tim stood, his hands full of amusements — this holiday, that little job. Her own sphere, if she were ready for all that, and only for all that. Why am I not resigned, Bea wondered — surely I ought to be? My friends at home, are they? But we do not discuss such things. Perhaps it is Eleanor, she thought, perhaps it is because she has always been there — somewhere else — that I haven't managed it. Have kept some little path open, always hoping to be able to run down it if I really needed to. But what a path — how could it still be open now? Paths: hers were all marked out.

The train slowed into a station, halted by flowers and benches and hot paving stones. Bea leant out of the window, reaching towards the scent of the flowers. It seemed a very peaceful place, a place to sit quietly in the sun. She stared back as the train moved off and the station swayed away round a bend; what trouble to have taken with a station, where no one lived or came, save to catch trains. She sat back in her seat, angry. They had taken such trouble and yet there was no trouble taken for her. For all those like her, to find a pleasant place for them. They had simply to be resigned, make themselves comfortable as they could. There were no niches for them: they would say, what? do you want a niche? well, haven't you had one, all these years? haven't you had it easy? It wasn't that she wanted it easy — Bea took out a cigarette, lit it; it was her last, she scrumpled the box and threw it out of the window: to hell, she thought, with their pleasant places — not easy, only possible. Somehow, though, she wasn't expected to want a place, any place — except Ada's, in the shade. There were no others. Displaced persons. Rootless middle-aged women of the middle-classes wandering the country murmuring, what can I do with my life. Damn it, I don't care how ridiculous it sounds, Bea muttered, flicking her ash violently to the floor.

The train was slowing again — this would be her station. It was larger, faintly littered, the benches uninviting.

'A bus? There's one goes round the villages in the afternoon. Leaves from the high street, half-an-hour or so,' he handed back her ticket, looking her up and down, 'or there's taxis.' A sneer came into his voice: 'Get there quicker by taxi.'

Bea snatched her ticket, 'I'm not that rich.' Which was not true, she thought, but damn his hatred. 'Where's the high street?' He pointed, grinning. Perhaps he does that to everyone, makes them all grind on to the bus stop hiding their wallets.

She stood in a newsagent's next to the bus stop. Should she buy Nellie cigarettes — she should buy her a carton, then. But she couldn't walk in with them in her hand, not after all this time, and just plonk them down. She bought as many packets as would fit into her bag. And now what am I going to do with these, she wondered, leave them casually scattered about? Perhaps we'll get through a lot, though, talking through the night. Bea smiled, the two of them hunched over a table stuffing cigarettes into their mouths, gesticulating, talking, lights burning. Dear god, she thought, I am looking forward to seeing her. I feel ill with waiting. She leant against the bus stop, her knees going soggy under her. No lunch, too many cigarettes. She pushed herself upright and walked carefully back to the newsagent's, bought a bar of chocolate, carried it back to the bus stop. Her handbag felt heavy, distended by cigarettes. She propped her back against the concrete post.

'Excuse me,' a woman stood in front of her — she had plumped her shopping down on the ground, a string bag sagged against her calves, brown paper leaning out of it. Bea looked at her. The woman moved a little closer, a little to one side. The string bag lurched to the pavement. The woman stared at her for a moment, 'You're leaning against the time-table, if you don't mind.'

Bea started away. She stood weakly behind the line of shopping bags, gripping her chocolate. The town seemed effortlessly alien. The bus came; she rescued a parcel of rubber gloves that fell from the other woman's string bag into the gutter. Inside she unwrapped the chocolate and ate it hurriedly, stuffing the foil and paper between the seats. She looked out of the window, feeling sick still, and bleary. The road ran between high hedgerows and then began to drop down into little villages, a hill down into each, a brief pause in some square by the war memorial and a climb out the other side. Bea peered anxiously at names, at shops as they passed. Finally the driver called down to her as they swung into another little square.

Here, then. She looked round — a street of shops lay off to her left. She turned down it. On the corner, a pub. The shop. It was across the road, painted green. Boxes of peaches in the window. Bea turned aside into the pub; she was not ready. She had not thought — of anything. Of what she should say. Would she be recognised, even — what if Nellie turned and said, and what can I do for you madam? Quite. She stood in the window, looking across — what if she came out now, it might be early closing. Bea finished her drink, and bought another. I'll just finish this, and then I'll go. Somewhere. The gin began to deaden the back of her head; she sat down on a stool, not to have to look at the shop door. I'm mad, she thought, staring into the dregs at the bottom of the glass, how am I going to get back home in time? And then put the glass carefully down on the bar and went out into the street.

The street was hot, but the inside of the shop cool and darker. She shut the door carefully behind her; a bell tinkled. Someone came out from the back of the shop, half glanced at her, turned towards the paper bags, 'What can I get —' Eleanor watched her hand drop slowly away from the paper bags. She turned around. 'Hello Bea,' she said.

Bea was looking at her slightly sideways, 'Hello.'

A short silence. 'You haven't come for fruit, I take it?' Eleanor's hand twitched towards the paper bags.

'Don't be silly, Nellie! I've come to see you.' She shifted her handbag in front of her, 'Is there somewhere I could sit down?'

Eleanor went out towards the back, 'Shall I put the kettle on for tea?'

Bea heard her climbing the stairs. She strayed over to the window and began fingering the peaches, turning them in their little compartments. Eleanor came back with the chairs. She watched as Bea sat back and reached into her handbag, took the cigarette Bea offered her, could say nothing, still.

Bea looked her up and down: 'That's a hideous overall, Nellie.'

'I'm too old for vanity. It's functional.'

'You're never too old for vanity, that's just an affectation of yours — for god's sake take it off.'

Eleanor inhaled, looking away, looking up at the cobwebs beginning to gather again in the corners. 'You don't like it because it makes me look like a shop assistant. I am a shop assistant, born and bred.'

Bea sighed: 'Any shop assistant with the opportunity to dress otherwise doesn't wear those things — they're what owners give them, to mark them down, as Lyons' girls, or whatever.' She flicked ash neatly into a heap next to her chair and looked up again to Eleanor's face, tilted towards the ceiling. 'Class games. You can't get away from me as easily as that, Nellie dear.'

Eleanor looked down, at her: 'Your having once chosen to come, after all this time?'

'Now that I am here.'

Eleanor shook her head slightly. She had not the extent of this, the breadth of it. Was this an afternoon, an odd afternoon — some gesture of — what? Reparation. Nostalgia. It could be nothing else; an afternoon in the old times. Had thinking about her brought her here? Had she been doing too much of that, Eleanor wondered. She felt almost compromised. As if it had been her that Bea had obeyed in coming here, not herself.

Bea looked into her lap; how the journey was laid across her skirt in pieces of lint, dim flakes of ash, chocolate. 'My having gone away,' she said quietly, 'it would follow that I would have to be the one to come back.' She fished out two more cigarettes and held one out towards Eleanor, still looking only towards her lap. It went lightly from between her fingers.

'Come back?' In the silence they could hear the wheeze of steam.

'Isn't that the kettle boiling?' said Bea.

Eleanor hung over the tea-pot, staring down into it; wasn't this odd, odder than she was letting herself know? Bea sitting down there, smoking a great deal in a navy blue suit, after almost twenty-five years. What could she be doing? Eleanor felt numbed. Perhaps it was some obscure need for symmetry, a pendulum swinging through quarter centuries. But that was clearly ridiculous. Her hand groped for the tea canister on the shelf — come back? There could be no coming back. But perhaps she has me on her conscience, because she left or because I never married, and it has worked on her until she needs to come — but if that's so, how will she get me off? I shall have to release her: you are not guilty. She spooned in the tea; that is all right, I suppose, she thought, gathering the biscuits onto the tray, since I have begun to see myself as guilty, guilty enough. Perhaps that's what she wants too, tell me it was my fault, Nellie. Or is it supposed to be all over? Eleanor paused at the top of the stairs. Surely it is only me that still turns it over and over. She will have moved on; it is dead for her, a memory. An episode caught up for ever with a certain period, a certain flavour: the fifties, girlish freedom, living a flirtation. A thing of the past. Eleanor's feet fell heavily on the stairs. She seemed to feel the lines of her face settling as she descended.

Bea turned from the window as she came in: 'You don't seem to have many customers.'

'It's not three yet – this is the after lunch lull, still. Lasts a long time in these places.'

Bea walked across the floor, her heels sounding on the boards. She stopped just beyond the mug that Eleanor held out to her, 'Won't you take your overall off? For your tea break? I can't see you properly, how you look.' She took the tea and sat down to look up at Eleanor.

'It's hardly my tea break, at this hour.' Eleanor stood, her hands by her sides, returning Bea's stare. This was nothing to Bea, she reminded herself; an afternoon, a memory momentarily reanimated, called into jerky life. To strut across a screen, a shadow puppet amusing for its very lifelessness. She turned away to pour out a mug of tea and paused, setting down the milk bottle. What was there for her in being obdurate? Like a lump of granite because she faced something slippery that would fade or leave in a moment? But what did that matter? Surely the granite had had its outing. She turned back, her hands going to the plastic overall buttons.

'Exhume the mummy, why not? Though we crumble when exposed to the air, you know.' She drew the overall off and laid it over her chair, thrust her hands into the pockets of her corduroy trousers. 'Well?'

Bea sat upright, mug on her lap, half turned in her chair. She took in the sagging brown cloth, the thin brown cotton shirt flapping around a concave body. 'But you're so thin!' she exclaimed; her hand strayed out towards Eleanor, as if to comfort those exposed bones. Eleanor stepped back; Bea looked up at her again, letting her hand fall. 'Don't touch the exhibits?'

Eleanor turned to her tea. 'I don't care for this line much,' she remarked. The skeleton is fragile after so long underground, yes; but do we have to say so? She sat down, offering the biscuits. Bea bent over them. 'You're quite grey,' she said suddenly.

Bea looked up: 'Have you only just noticed? I must have wonderful presence, to hide it for so long.'

They looked at each other, their faces close, each noting the detail of change. The eyes yellowing, the fall of the mouth's ends. Each briefly hating in the other these uglinesses, these signs of time's passing. And then they drew back, drawing away from a mutual hostility.

'You are eating those biscuits,' Eleanor observed.

'No lunch, only some chocolate on the bus – could I have more tea?

I'll pour it.'

Eleanor looked round at Bea as she lifted the lid enquiringly. 'Didn't you come by car, Bea?'

'No, train and then a bus from the town, why?'

'There isn't a bus back, that's all. You'll have to ring a taxi.'

Bea opened her bag and brought out a cigarette packet; the light caught on the cellophane of other packets within, unopened.

'What a lot of cigarettes you carry!'

Bea gestured vaguely, holding out the open packet towards her: 'I thought we might get through a lot, that's all.'

Eleanor was silent, holding the cigarette in the palm of her hand. A woman came through the shop door and she laid the cigarette on the seat of her chair.

'Not wearing your overall, Miss Hardy?'

'Thought I'd give it a rest,' Eleanor said.

'I'll have a pound of those English plums. You do get tired of wearing the same thing always, don't you.'

Eleanor handed her her change: 'Be back in it tomorrow I expect.' She turned back to Bea as the door closed, 'You see? You've upset my customers. They expect an overall — it tells them who I am.'

'And if you weren't wearing it they might notice who you really are, you mean.'

Eleanor grinned, picking up the cigarette she had left: 'I don't think they're as interested as all that.' She took the matches from her overall pocket; already she was smoking too much. Bea thought they might get through a lot? The air was thick with hints, intimations, references to something — as if Bea had a key, or perhaps a plan, that she had missed. Eleanor walked across the room to a carton of plums and turned them between her hands. She began to pick out rotten ones, throwing them into an empty box at her feet. The work had a rhythm and pleasure to it. Her back was to Bea; 'What train'll you be catching?' she asked. She went on with the plums, hearing only the crinkling noise of the biscuit packet behind her. There were no more spoilt plums; her hands came to rest on the edge of the carton, still for a moment. Then she took the matches from her pocket and lit the cigarette she held at one corner of her mouth. She turned, to see Bea examining her biscuit, holding it out, away from her.

Bea looked over: 'I'm becoming long-sighted — wondered what it had written on it.' She put the biscuit down, 'Do you want me to go, then?'

Eleanor considered that; the answer, she thought, was almost yes, of course – as quickly as possible. For the fruitlessness of it, the irrelevance of this episode to the past and future alike. And yet – that seemed not to be everything. She was curious, desperately curious. For she had so little to go on, there was so much she wanted to know. Since Ann and Dee the possibilities had grown, she had had to see that; the possibilities she had turned away from. And those fragile little ideas – she wanted to flesh them out. To know something of how she might have been. What would she lose, living it now, for once?

'No,' she said at last, 'but I'd like to know when you are.'

Bea sat back in her chair. She felt drained, even though, she realised, she had not kept herself up to a pitch of seriousness. It is so long, I have perhaps forgotten how – to say what I mean. But is it necessary? She knows. I don't want to go, she thought, not yet. 'I really hadn't thought about it – going, I mean. I just came.' She stared across at Eleanor; they both stared.

'You just came?'

Bea nodded. She bent and swept biscuit crumbs from her skirt, 'If I rang up Tim – could I stay for a few days?'

'As long as you like.'

Eleanor moved forward with relief to serve as the shop door swung open.

The light was beginning to fade from the front room. Eleanor stood at the window, looking down on the street, on the lights of the pub beginning to spill out into the evening, putting out daylight. Behind her the bottle of gin wrapped in brown paper that Bea had fetched. She could hear her now in the kitchen sorting through the glasses. And yet the sense of invasion was dulled – why was that, Eleanor wondered. Because Bea did not wander about the room touching things, picking them up, letting them drop, asking little questions, do you still play the violin? Was that why, that she knew how to contain herself in the face of objects, the marks of a separate life – only that?

Or was it that she wanted it, now, as much as she could get: a great swell of invasion, a drowning rush of her. Good grief, Eleanor muttered to herself, thrusting her hands further into her armpits; aren't I carrying myself away now? That would be the end of it, a fitting, traditional end:

after so long carefully staked against the tide, firm and unwavering and above it, seeing – to be swept off, letting go, going under, all pent-up released and out of control.

She felt Bea behind her now. 'Did you find anything?' she asked.

'Well, yes – though you do hide your less sober glass, don't you?'

Eleanor turned: 'Less sober glass?'

'To drink out of.' Bea straightened, holding out a drink. Eleanor was silhouetted against the window, a tall thin figure blurred by rough daubs of fabric. It was that, somehow, for which she had not been prepared: Eleanor now skeletal, almost unworldly.

'Why are you so thin?' she demanded, the ice in the glass rattling.

'It affects many women like that, especially childless ones,' Eleanor said mildly, turning away again.

'What does?'

Eleanor put out a hand to the window frame, ran her hand slowly along the ridged wood – carefully as if exploring it. She had heard the fear in Bea's voice and she held it, there at the window, for a moment before answering. 'Not cancer, so far as anyone knows. Only old age, less appetite.'

Bea settled herself in an armchair, looking around at the darkening room, the mess of bottles and the bowl of ice-cubes. Do I parody myself, she wondered wearily, creating the materials for gin and tonic wherever I go – as if this were a hotel, and the bottle made it home? Someone else's stereotype, I don't drink that much. And I haven't been to a hotel in England for years.

'Did you ring your husband?'

'From the pub. He could hear the noise of carousing in the background. He was so surprised that he couldn't think of anything to say except, you haven't your night things with you. He is being very tolerant of my whims at the moment,' Bea paused to light a cigarette, 'but then why not? I have been a faithful, imaginative and charming wife to him. She's restless? Wants to go off visiting old friends? Give her a bit of rope, then. She won't do any harm –' Bea lapsed into silence. There was really no point to this, she thought, railing on against Tim. It had nothing to do with him. If this were a speech, an anniversary, say, she could even say that he had been a faithful, imaginative, charming husband. That would cover it well enough, with a little licence, a few allowances that anyone must make for anyone else. She sighed, drawing the bottle across the table towards her. What was

111

she doing here, leaving Tim to grope about in the freezer for something to eat, buying bottles of gin in brown paper, yelling down pay-phones while hungry locals slid greasy smiles at her along the bar?

She started, seeing Eleanor appearing suddenly at the table; she had forgotten her, almost, leaning there in the window.

Eleanor frowned down, 'Did you come here to complain about your husband? Is that what this is for?'

'That's a little ruthless of you, Nellie.' Bea scooped ice-cubes into her glass.

'Does "ruthless" have anything to do with us at all? Do you think it can mean anything for you and me after —' Eleanor brought herself up short. If this were only a retreat for her. She should have realised how little Bea's presence had to do with her, had to do with where she was. It was where she was not, that mattered. She brought her glass down slowly to the table and poured another drink.

'I think perhaps that I don't mind being used as a refuge so long as I know that that is what is happening,' she said, enunciating the words carefully. For she was taut, waiting for that confirmation. The carapace set to lock in on itself; this time, she thought, I shall close off carefully with precision. I have been flinging myself open and shut as if she could touch me and I take it in my stride — enough of that, flapping open on the chance of a sop, a moment of reminiscence. Its relevance does matter. What would I do with some fragment of meaning, torn out of nowhere?

'I'm not taking refuge from Tim,' Bea looked up bleakly, 'there's nothing to take refuge from in him.'

Eleanor stood still, flat and black in front of her.

'If you want to know what I'm running away from, it's death. My mother-in-law's death.' And she began to laugh suddenly.

The room was dimmed with smoke. Bea had come to rest again in her armchair, amid the egg-rimmed plates. It was Nellie who always cooked omelettes in times of crisis, Bea remembered, for the therapeutic properties of breaking eggs. You can't without. This was a crisis for her then, and yet she seemed calm — or was it only that she seemed limber, easy in her soft shoes, limp clothes? It was all very controlled; had it always been Nellie in control, had she always felt so at sea? This was her ground, she hadn't realised in coming here how much it was, Eleanor's mind-ground. Where she seemed to know what it was that she wanted. I should have expected that, Bea thought. What was all that about, the life of the mind I was missing, if not this path-charting, signs of it strewn about casually as she speaks, little maps thrust into my hand. Bea leaned back heavily into her chair. So she sees where I am now.

Eleanor let her head rest against the window frame. 'I can't help you, Bea,' she said. She understood, yes. She saw into Bea's misery, and she had sat there at the table drawing out the threads from her, strand by strand, until the whole, the whole neat tapestry, lay between them. Its patches of colour: Ada's solemn, deliberate presence; the women in the agencies saying, you are not serious, we do not recognise you. And then she had thought her part performed, finished in the listening. Like for those who spread it out for you carefully, every detail: it hangs there a moment and then they have wrapped it away, begun to bustle, get on. It can't be helped, they say absently, already resigned. But she wants more of me, thought Eleanor dully, more. Not enough that I should see, understand. It is outrageous, that she should want me to provide some key, an outlet. The right phrase. What can she want me to say, why don't you leave your husband, Bea, is that it? How can she ask me for the word, a password, when that life of hers was built on my back? I shall do nothing. She eats away at me, just sucking blood for her own needs. Nothing.

She turned to the room, and walked quietly over to the armchair. She laid a hand along its back and looked down; Bea raised her head.

'I don't have a solution to your problem,' Eleanor said flatly.

Bea leaned forward and took a cigarette, thrusting one over her head at Eleanor; so that when Bea flicked her lighter Eleanor must bend to it, level with her eyes.

'I want to be able to talk to you, Nellie,' Bea said then, 'to talk. Not engage you as my psychoanalyst. Not talk to a wall. I am not asking just for your help.'

'What, then?'

Bea shrugged: 'I don't know, partly that. Partly I want you to talk to me.' She paused, inhaled, 'Stop trying to intimidate me, Nellie — if you don't want me here, I'll go, that's all.'

Eleanor began to wander about the room, idly touching the ornaments on the shelves. 'I don't want you to go, I want to know what you want —' she wheeled round and came back to where Bea still sat, washed up, her shoes off, in the armchair, 'you're the same as you always were, damn it — I think I know where you are and then you say, that's not it, and you never say what is it after all.'

Bea grinned through the smoke: 'I thought you didn't get overwrought and wave your arms around any more. I'll tell you what I want. I want you not to stand off from me any more.'

Eleanor sat down on the edge of the table. Her thigh met the cold china of the bowl where the ice-cubes had dissolved into grey dimpled water. She was aware of reaching the end of something, she did not know yet what. A long evening, the end of a long evening, she thought vaguely. Bea has been drinking gins, all evening. Lowers your resistance, hers and mine. How tiring it is to stand off, as she calls it. How tempting to lie down. She formulated a sentence carefully; the system felt fragile, as if it might run out of control at the next blow, quite out of control. She might say anything. 'That's quite something,' she said, 'I think I want to think about that, in the light of day.'

'There are toothbrushes for sale in the village.'

'Don't be pompous, Nellie, you can see I need other things. I can't live in this god-forsaken suit.' Bea eyed her across the table, 'Is there some reason why you don't want me to go?'

Eleanor laughed, reaching herself an extra slice of toast: 'You'll miss meeting my shop assistant, that's all. But she's coming to dinner anyway — you can do the shopping for me — with her lover.'

Bea lowered her cup, 'To dinner? Oh god, Nellie —' She stopped. Life went on, Eleanor's own separate life. What should she say, that she must have all her attention, that she must cancel everything, draw down the blinds? But she had assumed that, she realised, spreading marmalade absently across her toast. That Nellie would be free merely to bring herself to bear. She was not, after all, so unencumbered — that was a property of that fantasy figure, the mythical alternative Eleanor, who would always come when you needed her. Like superman, no home life to get in the way. She had spread the marmalade very carefully, she saw, to the edges of the toast; the way it had to be before Ginny would eat any, those long tortuous breakfasts ago. Who did one ever cancel everything for? Family illness. Death, and the time the cat had got lost and had to be looked for, every waking moment. All in the family. And I'm not asking that, am I, she thought, that she should put me first like that.

Eleanor was watching her, watching her biting her lip, calling back protest. Yes, of course Bea thought I would be available for her, any time she

114

wanted me. She has always taken me for granted. Eleanor let her resentment flow out: 'This one never wears an overall,' she said, 'and I have been to supper with them. As far as I can tell their manners should not distress you too much.'

Bea flushed for a moment, lighting a cigarette: 'I'm not sure I feel equal to dinner-time conversation, that's all.' She looked over angrily. Eleanor was grinning to herself over a scrap of paper by her plate. 'You do like to bait me, don't you? Such an easy target.'

Eleanor looked up: 'That doesn't necessarily make it less worth hitting. Here, that's the list. And here,' she delved into her pocket, 'are the keys to the van. Blue Ford, parked in the alley at the back. I have to open the shop soon — but it's early closing day. If you're back around lunchtime we could go for a walk in the afternoon, or something.' She got up from the table and then stood uncertainly there for a moment. 'Is that all right?' she said finally.

'Yes of course,' Bea said quickly, glancing up.

Eleanor still hung, leaning at the table. 'Forgive me if I'm just venting empty spleen on you, Bea. Perhaps I haven't had anyone to tease for too long.'

Bea picked up the car keys and swung them between her fingers. 'I'll tell you,' she said at last, 'when I think we're not even.'

Eleanor was bundling up sheets of newspaper in the shop when Bea went through. She paused in the rear doorway: 'Last night, you said I'd have to get a taxi to the station — now I find you've a car. Wouldn't you have taken me?'

Eleanor stood with the clumsy armful of crinkled, yellowing newspapers. 'I would have taken you,' she said, 'but you couldn't've counted on it, could you, when you came? I wanted to know how much you'd planned, I suppose.'

'Scheming to keep me here?'

Eleanor stooped to thrust the newspapers onto a low shelf. Then she turned to the door, the blind still rolled down over it. She began to roll the canvas up. 'Yes, I suppose I was, Beatrice.'

Bea waited in the doorway, but Eleanor did not go on; she stood at the door, the half-rolled blind in her hand. 'I'll see you at lunchtime,' Bea said, and Eleanor heard her footsteps receding to the back door.

Dee arrived a few minutes later; Eleanor looked at her vaguely, as if seeing her through mist. The familiar yellow hair, the hunched shoulders; it was after all the same Dee, she thought — but what shall I say to her? It was as if she were standing at the bottom of some vast round valley, alone. All around there were things to look at — things she must look at — things she must look at and find out about. But explain all this to Dee, who was far away, all of a sudden? Eleanor could not see how it was begun.

Dee looked her over, standing absently in the doorway: 'You look tousled,' she said.

Eleanor's hand went to her hair, 'Do I?' She crossed the room, 'I've forgotten to put my overall on, you mean.' She shrugged herself into it, felt for the cigarettes in the pocket. The mechanisms of the day reemerged out of the mist: 'How about a smoke before the rush?'

Dee sat on the step, and waited. Eleanor so easily became unfathomable — from one day to the next she seemed without certainties, Dee thought. She'll reveal herself, come out to you — all kinds of strangenesses there for the asking. And then she'll clam up again, she thinks you're young, empty-headed, stuffed with arrogance, blue-prints for a world you know nothing about. I can't deny some of that, she thought, but better inaccurate blue-prints than no blue-prints at all. They always seemed to be having that argument. Strange that Eleanor shouldn't be drawing up some sort of blue-print, somewhere secretly. How could she live like this, seeing things, and not say, that has to change? For she didn't (and wasn't that the alternative?) say, I'm not going to look any more, things are too bad. She glanced sideways: Eleanor sat immobile on the upturned crate, her eyes on the patch of pavement in front of the shop doorway. She must be able to consider herself apart from it all, from everybody — I forget that, Dee thought, being so used to thinking of myself as part of a huge mass. Doesn't Eleanor see how anyone would look at her, the categories they would use? Female, they would say. But for Eleanor that's just a category, not necessarily an inferior one. She isn't listening to that. Dee threw her cigarette butt out into the gutter; but how can she be satisfied with that old individual approach? It's so easy: see me as I see myself. And such nonsense.

Still nothing said; she looked over again. She felt a kind of lightness, a vacuum between them. The tension that so often held her, making her move about the shop conscious of every gesture, as if there were a camera trained on her — this morning that had gone. Dee stood up quietly; she had been so expecting its presence that she had taken it for granted, had

116

been sitting, smoking, as if under the microscope. But — Eleanor really was not aware of her, she realised. She walked back into the shop, experiencing this as a physical release: she began to dance, a muted tap-dance, her hands in her pockets.

The dance was absorbing, she shuffled from one side of the room to the other, humming to herself. And then she came to rest, absently picking an apple from a box and biting into it. She looked over at the doorway, where Eleanor still sat — what am I here for though, if not to be noticed, aren't I deliberately exposing myself? She went back to the doorway; it was disconcerting. She could see now that Eleanor was quite abstracted. Completely withdrawn.

'There'll be some customers coming soon, I expect,' she said at Eleanor's elbow.

Eleanor looked round at her and quickly down the street: people had begun to issue from doorways all along. 'Yes,' she said, and stood to carry the crate back inside the door.

Dee turned to the window, to the bunches of bananas and grapes hung there; she touched them lightly and looked out past them into the street. She couldn't hover like this in the window, as if not here. If this were another woman, one who wasn't twenty years older, Dee thought, I would say something. At least find out if she wanted me to go or stay, leave her alone or not. Dee thrust her hands into her pockets: and I don't, not because I'm frightened of her, her sharpness — that's an excuse. She turned round — Eleanor was checking over the change in the till. Perhaps I am right not to trust her, she thought. Twenty years may really be such a barrier that honesty across it is impossible. Perhaps it is better not to risk it, to keep hold of what we have and to feel our way slowly. But it should be different — I should trust her. She turned back to the street — it was too much, she couldn't act like that, a great leap in the dark for the sake of how things ought to be.

A string of customers began to come into the shop, then, and Dee smiled at them extravagantly, guiltily, these women that she could not trust or help. She packed carrots into the corners of a shopping bag with delicacy, counted change slowly into an old woman's hand. She could hear across the room faint starts of conversation as Eleanor showed someone the pears, how hard they were. 'So you're wearing your overall again this morning then,' she heard, and looked up as the door closed. Eleanor's mouth had crumpled away from a smile and she stood gazing at the door,

117

her hand playing with one of the overall buttons.

Dee crossed over the room, 'What's the matter, Eleanor, what is it?' She stopped in front of her, unsure again.

But Eleanor looked down, and at her, her eyes slowly moving over Dee's face. Finally she smiled a little: 'Yes, I'm a little unsettled. Bea turned up to see me yesterday afternoon.'

'How's that? After all this time?'

Eleanor looked over her head, towards the door, remembering that she had come through it, the bell tinkling. 'Well, I don't know,' she turned to the vegetables, began to straighten the boxes, 'I don't know how it is and I don't know why she's here.' So it could become part of what went on, then; Eleanor was relieved, that she could speak about it after all. 'She's gone into town to get the shopping, you'll see her tonight – you are coming, aren't you?'

'Well, yes, unless you'd like to put it off.' Dee grinned, for she thought she saw again an appraising look.

'No, I don't think so – I'd like to see how you all get on.'

Ann swung open the door of the wardrobe and looked at herself in the mirror. Then she went through into Dee's room next door: Dee was in front of her cupboard, twitching unhappily at the hanging shirts.

'Do you think I look appropriate?' Ann asked.

Dee turned her head briefly: 'I wish I knew what was appropriate.' The problem of appearance oppressed her: for whom was she dressing? The idea of having seriously to modify her style of dress for Bea's benefit annoyed and confused her –if it wasn't herself that she was exhibiting, then who was it?

Ann settled herself in the doorway to watch. Dee, she thought, allowed herself to be too malleable. Had to go through this agony all the time of searching for the right compromise.

'Why don't you wear what you want,' she said. It wasn't as if there were collars and ties and brylcreem to be decently kept from Bea. Even if there were though, if I really thought that only those garments expressed me, shouldn't I wear them, she wondered. Letting them see it how it was. But it seemed an impossible question to answer, the problems of explaining that painful uniform so immense already – how could one hope to wear it, actually, and be understood.

Dee had strewn things about the bed. Wear what I want, yes; Ann is right. Too easy to slip back into thinking I must disguise myself in order to be acceptable. Only now I don't know what it is I do want to wear. She glanced over at Ann: 'Strikes me you look a little as if you're trying to be Romaine Brooks.'

Ann grinned: 'Do you think so?' She moved to look at herself again in Dee's mirror. 'I just look small dark and distinguished,' she said happily. The prospect of Bea was exciting. Would she know what to make of her? Romaine Brooks junior. It would be a pleasure to embarrass this Beatrice. 'Do you think she's staying?' she asked. Dee seemed hardly to be listening, absorbed in peeling things on and off. 'I suppose she can't be,' she went on, 'given what she'd lose. It isn't often done, at any rate — and it seems a bit late for the big leap.'

Dee considered the effect of a scarf, unknotted it and picked up another: 'Do you think women who aren't feminists make that leap very often? It seems like too much horror to be worthwhile — no one else thinks it's the thing to do and you don't either. That seems to have been why they didn't stay together in the first place, doesn't it? She's hardly going to change her mind now, still no doubt believing in family life and not particularly in women. And with all that to lose.' Dee folded another scarf precisely and tried it, 'I think that's why Eleanor is upset — the pointlessness of it all.' Dee realised that she was angry with Bea — for having gone off and married in the first place, and now for coming back to parade her other life in front of Eleanor. How could she help doing so?

Ann surveyed Dee's final choice: 'That's very fine, are you liking it?'

Dee still looked in the mirror doubtfully: 'I don't make Bea sound very nice, do I?' she said. The clothes would do all right, she decided. She followed Ann down the stairs, vaguely troubled. She should be leaving Bea alone — how could she stand in judgement on her from this quite different place? Or there again, how not? Was there any point pretending that she didn't have a side to take, think Bea had been wrong to leave Eleanor, pronouncing them doomed. Sealing their fate. Think she should have stayed even if it would have been for what she thought were the wrong reasons, or not reason enough. Faith would have done, she should have had faith. But this personal hostility that she felt, making her feet fall heavy on the stairs? Was that part, too, of having a political view? How did it go with some attempt — and Dee felt that she made it, quite deliberately — to understand the conditions of others' actions,,of others' views? That was all hopeless, or an intellectual veneer, underneath she just hated the ones who

119

chose differently?

She watched Ann take the bottle of wine from the kitchen table, followed her out of the door and into the lane. She stopped to latch the gate and look up and down. The council had sent out a machine to cut back the hedges: they were bare and spiky, browning leaves and grass lying on the verges; all the flowers had been cut, even the hawthorn was bare, the inner branches revealed, scarred by the blades. Perhaps it isn't worth living in the country, Dee thought, looking at the mess of chopped foliage, even if it grows back better than before, I don't want to see it.

Ann had walked off ahead, but she waited for Dee at the corner. 'What's the matter?' she asked, seeing Dee scuffing pebbles angrily as she walked.

Dee waved her arm round: 'Look at the hedges! They look like one of those tinsely paper things you put round christmas cakes — all bent in at the middle and tufted at the top.' She took Ann's arm and leant into her a little, letting herself be carried along. 'It's Bea really, I keep finding myself condemning her out of hand and I feel I shouldn't,' she said.

'Jealous, perhaps,' Ann said mildly.

'What does he do?' Bea twitched at a napkin; they were limp, even seemed to smell faintly from having been so long in a drawer.

Eleanor came down the corridor. 'What does who do?' she asked, putting glasses on the edge of the table.

'Your assistant's lover, I mean.'

'I didn't tell you, did I.' Eleanor looked her up and down, her head on one side. Such a silly game to be playing, she thought. What will she think, that I'm trying to compromise her? She might refuse to meet them — but she's too well-bred. She can just be rude to them both. She turned back to the table: 'You've brought out those old serviettes, Bea — don't they smell, or anything? I don't use them.'

Bea sighed, 'What do you wipe your fingers on when you're not wearing an overall?' She began to go round the table, taking them away.

Eleanor was searching through a cupboard, 'There are some paper ones here, I think.'

'Are they very young?' Bea asked, 'Are they both going to come in jeans and wipe their fingers on them?'

Eleanor drew her head out of the cupboard to stare curiously at her: 'You're not really worried about that, are you?'

Bea left the table abruptly and threw herself into a chair. She stared over at the curtains, green-patterned. Her eyes seemed full of tears: it was so wearing, all this between them. And why was Eleanor on this young couple's side then, and against her? At home, thick linen napkins. 'The point is, I'm not wearing dirty jeans. I'm wearing a skirt which I bought because you said you were having people to dinner and I thought —' Bea stopped herself, she was almost wailing. So very tiring. And she wanted to blend in. 'Shall I put on the trousers I bought?' she said, leaning forward.

Eleanor closed the cupboard to stand over her, 'You look very charming. They'll like you like that.' She pressed a bundle of paper into Bea's hand: 'I found these, for our fingers. I'm sure we'll need them.'

'What does he do then, this young man, that I'm supposed to find unpalatable? What do you think I automatically disapprove of?'

Eleanor grinned and reached two cigarettes from the packet on the table, lit them, handed one down to Bea. 'They'll be here in a minute,' she said, 'Dee's lover Ann is an artist.'

Bea stared, then her eyes flickered over her clothes and back to Eleanor's face. They watched each other.

Why am I putting us through all this? Only to prove that more than what she is divides us? To show her that she can't use me unless I allow the differences to go under for a while. How if we have things in common it is because I allow it, put myself where she is. But when she sees that, what then? If she can't take me for granted, Eleanor thought, perhaps she won't take me at all.

Bea let the thing hang in front of her: as sudden and violent as a blow. Here was the other life, Eleanor's separate life, then; and Eleanor throwing it at her, waiting for it to be thrust aside. She reached out and grabbed Eleanor's wrist, 'You should have told me before, you bastard.' She shook the thin arm fiercely. Always coming back to the same place, as if she could take back that old decision, now. So this was what Eleanor's paths had led her to. 'I hope they're not twenty-five years younger,' she grinned up, 'there but for the grace of god?'

Eleanor looked back steadily: 'More or less,' she said.

Bea lifted herself wearily out of her chair. Everything had been said already — it was all done. Now she had to sit through while these two young women fleshed out their life. And what had it to do with her — that was the point perhaps, that she should see the details of how it was not her life and couldn't ever be. Teach your grandmother to suck eggs, she thought angrily, folding the paper napkins onto plates. I know just what I am already, do you think something has escaped me?

They came into the room behind Eleanor. Bea glanced quickly between them: my daughters' generation, she thought, what can they not think of doing? And called that back, so much was the same; it could not be so easy an answer, that these two did it because it was possible? Bea looked at them: an air of defiance almost palpable, a shiny film around them; if they were wrong, and it were not possible?

She moved towards them, smiling. Ann took the greeting, the warm colours of Bea's clothes, took them together politely as if holding them a little apart in front of her, as if also to give Bea for a moment the benefit of the doubt, and smiled in return.

Dee stood back; as Eleanor stooped over the remains of the gin Dee stood beside her, taking the offered glass slowly, her glance going between Bea, seen now from the side, appraising Ann's costume (they would be talking about Romaine Brooks, Dee thought) and Eleanor, looking doubtfully at a small row of tonic bottles.

'I don't think there'll be enough,' she was saying, 'Bea drinks too much.'

'She won't be able to, then, will she,' Dee remarked.

'Ah, she'll only drink it neat,' and Eleanor smiled. 'I'd better distribute these — Ann does drink gin?'

Dee nodded, 'And she's flirting with Beatrice.'

Eleanor paused, and looked Dee over carefully. 'My dear Dee, so do you and I, if that's what you want to call it.'

'Do we? Not like that!' She gestured over: Bea and Ann were laughing.

Eleanor shrugged: 'They're playing party games, that's all.'

'You're damn cheerful all of a sudden.'

Eleanor put the glasses down again on the table and took a packet of cigarettes from her pocket. She shook them until Dee smiled and took one. 'What's the matter?' Eleanor asked when they were lit, 'Do you want to as well?' She watched as Dee thought round her answers, considering how much she should dare. This is an odd conversation for us to be having, she thought, I didn't know we'd got this far. And perhaps we haven't, she added, feeling Dee's fright as she smoked carefully through her cigarette.

'No, I don't,' Dee said slowly, and paused again. 'I suppose it's that I wanted to keep you to myself, and now she's here —'

Eleanor stared — who had released all this, she wondered. Dee blushing here and Bea across the room wrapping her charm all over Ann. It must be Bea and I, we have generated it. She felt the current running between herself and Dee, smiled to her: 'The prodigal daughter. But not come to repent, I don't think.'

Dee watched her carrying the drinks across the room, feeling light and drained, as if careful needles had rid her of so much excess fluid. Eleanor is cheerful, she thought vaguely, there's no getting away from that. She finished the cigarette; but she is speaking to me again. And this Beatrice, here in the flesh — perhaps it means that I can say anything. As if she had made Eleanor nearer, more like us. Sex, Dee thought, Beatrice has brought sex with her.

Eleanor made room for herself abruptly beside Bea: 'You mustn't monopolise Ann,' she said, 'and Dee could do with your conversation — you've been neglecting her.'

Bea moved warily across the room. Seeing Dee's stillness, a look that lengthened the gap between them, she realised that she was bound into the gathering, that her presence had significance for everyone there. Not a spectator, after all; they expect me to be a protagonist. She looked at Dee's broad flat face. Like an avenging angel, but older than Ginny. Perhaps she gives all heterosexual women that look, or shouldn't I have spoken to Ann? A corner of Bea's mouth lifted; always the same fears.

'So you're Dee,' she said, offering a cigarette. Dee took one, and nodded. 'You looked a little like the recording angel as I came over.'

'I tend to appear judgemental unintentionally.'

'When you don't mean it to show?' So they knew about her and Nellie.

'Sometimes I even try not to judge.' Dee spoke abruptly. How had she lapsed so quickly into this need to justify herself?

'But before I came over you had decided against me on the basis of my past history?' Bea looked down at her, all at once angry, as if this were an injustice she cared about.

I should answer. Cannot always be refusing to answer, Dee thought. Perhaps she will still be listening. A bit of self-exposure. 'What else is there to judge from?' She waved a hand to forestall the answer, 'I can see and sympathise with all your reasons for acting as you did, for the reasons that women have always succumbed to pressure. But I still judge your action as wrong — or I wouldn't have done what I did myself, believing in it as the right thing to do.' Dee looked round her for the ashtray.

'Things were different then,' Bea said shortly.

'It couldn't seem the right thing to do?' Dee nodded, 'I know — and yet some did. And anyway — you didn't want to believe it was right, did you — it was too inconvenient.'

'Perhaps those that did do it then did it for less upright reasons than you.'

'Too warped for anything else, you mean?' Dee rooted angrily in her trouser pocket for another cigarette, 'And we none of us do it by choice? I do, Beatrice, I wouldn't bolster up your heterosexual world at any price — not for any lack of ability to enjoy sex with men, or their company, or their money, or their protection.' Dee found that her hands shook over the matchbox as she struggled to light her cigarette, head down over it.

Bea looked down at this fumbling figure: not so easy for her, either. But she would not let her get away with this rewriting of things. 'We didn't have it before us as a cause, so much, then. I didn't feel I was betraying anyone else by not doing it.' She flicked her lighter and held it out to Dee, 'But of course that's how it seems to you.'

Dee shrugged: 'Easy to say that now, I suppose.'

'And what were you doing in the fifties?'

Dee shook her head, 'All right. I only became a lesbian when we all did, in the women's movement. Easy then to think it was the logical step —'

Bea listened: to Dee, she thought, that had been one of those moments when one briefly has control over life. The choice is made and you go under in the rush of consequences, coming up somewhere far downstream, the scenery on either side not what you expected, the details no one has warned you about. But Dee seems to think the unexpected worth dealing with. And if you don't like your surroundings? Can you start over, or only be borne on? However I put it, she thought, the answer seems the same, weighed down as I am. And if it were possible I should still have to have room enough to see where else I might like to go — and I don't see my way. She stepped aside slightly so that she could see Eleanor, gesticulating in a corner with Ann. It seemed incredible, for a moment, that Eleanor should be so close, in the same room — for shouldn't she have been some great way off? And so she is, Bea reminded herself, somewhere quite else — these geographical metaphors — and yet in the same room. She smiled across: if this was the only journey that had come to her, perhaps she had only to realise what it was she was wanting from it.

124

'This is an odd gathering,' Ann said, surveying the table. Eleanor lifted her head from a dish of vegetables; it has caught her too, she thought, we are all speaking in provocations, chipping away at a thin surface. We shall say too much, not be able to face each other, most likely. Perhaps that's why we do it – so that it shouldn't happen again. For it is odd, a strain on us. Odd what it does for Bea – here she is drawn into some relationship with me, is not Tim's wife at all. 'In what sense?' she asked.

Ann backed off a little: 'I meant in terms of age, mainly –'

Dee broke in: 'No, no, it's not odd.' She gestured at the table, so full of dishes and glass, 'This is obviously a symbolic act, nothing to do with how we live from day to day.' She grinned at Bea, 'Like going home for christmas.' Dee paused to drink from her glass, wanting her words to reach them both. They might not want to listen. But what they might do affected her, now, had come away from the vague mass of the world safely outside and become what the women around her were doing. Her surroundings. Did they realise that, she wondered, what that meant? Her politics, her beliefs, what she went on throwing at them – they were fragile. She couldn't go on if some answering flash of recognition didn't meet her somewhere, somewhere amongst them. She had to ask that of them.

Her voice sounded loud, 'If we actually met more frequently – that might mean something. Be odd, if you like. People choosing to meet often are.'

'Does that mean that chance meetings are worthless?' Bea asked.

'Of course not – but they have their limitations. And they stay just there – only chance meetings.'

Bea shrugged: it was as if she were being confronted by the initiates of some ancient cult, who spoke to outsiders across a great enigmatic gulf. 'You ask a great deal,' she said. Dee nodded.

'They do think themselves wonderful, don't they – telling me what I should have done, what I should do now – do they have my whole life mapped out? A lesson in one of their feminist books?' Bea halted in her sweep round the room, brought up against the dim glow of the windows. She looked down at the grey street: 'The street lights have gone out,' she said.

Eleanor stretched out in the armchair, 'It's late, that's all.'

Bea stood still, staring out. 'Do they do that to you, Nellie, tell you where you went wrong?'

Eleanor, considering, saw how in fact they kept clear of that intrusion. They take me as I am, she thought, as if I made sense to them. 'No,' she said slowly, 'they don't. They think of me — as a survivor.' She reached out to the cigarette packet that lay close by on the table, 'Someone whose actions have been necessary.' She lit a cigarette in the silence. 'Perhaps the thing is that they wonder whether they could have done what I did. And they can see themselves being you.'

Bea leaned her back against the window frame: 'There seems to be this idea —perhaps they passed it on to you, Nellie — that my life is some sort of soft option,' her voice dropped, Eleanor could hardly hear, 'easy and worthless.' She had crossed the room to Eleanor's chair in a sudden movement, 'Do you think it's so easy, trying to live within it all, do you? Having to do all those things, exactly what is expected? Do you think it's so easy, trying to make your family feel as if they're real, individual people who matter, while all the time you must stay within every bond of convention there is?' She turned aside again, to the window. 'How much easier to lend your life significance with a little non-conformity.'

Eleanor eased her stiff shoulders into the chair back. None of this is addressed to me, she thought, not me personally. But that seemed not to matter, that Bea stood railing against her accusers almost unaware of her presence, it was enough that she was speaking at last.

'Your conformity means more to other people than my failure to measure up,' she said, 'I simply cease to exist to the world and you have your place in it. Whether you or I think our own lives have meaning is something else.'

Bea turned her head briefly, blankly; she had moved on. Worthless, they dared to call her life worthless. All that care over so long. She frowned — better not to go into that just now. 'Bringing up my daughters was not worthless,' she said to the window. She was aware of a strange rigidity in her body as if she were really in some dock, verdict about to be read out, and steeling herself to show them, the prosecutors, nothing. These three women, on the fringe of nowhere. What should I care, she thought, for their ignorant condemnation. But she stood strained to penetrate the silence around Eleanor's chair: was she with them, then, that there was no sound but the drag of an ashtray across the table?

Eleanor ground out the stub of her cigarette; words were coming suddenly into her mind. As if she were released from some paralysis by Bea's relapse from control and certainty, as if only now were she able to speak to Bea on her own terms. 'All that doesn't really concern them, Bea, they weren't thinking of what you have or haven't done with yourself, of your day-to-day struggle – they weren't saying any of that was worthless. All they really said was that it was lousy of you to have left me.' She drew out another cigarette: 'And they might be right about that.'

'We had so much to lose, Nellie –' Bea looked over, reading the challenge in Eleanor's silence. And yet now that they were at last speaking of it she felt a great relief. She spread her hands: 'I was twenty-five – I'd been in love often enough before – hadn't you? I knew it didn't last – that we'd become indifferent, friends, perhaps. Nothing wrong with that – but to throw off everything else in the world for it?' She left the window, trailing her hand across the pane, moving away to the end of the room, to the bookcase where the light hardly penetrated. 'I didn't see it as those two do, all part of their plan for changing the world. Some sort of radical alternative. I hardly saw it as different at all, like marrying a woman instead of a man – except all the trouble it would cause. It wasn't an issue then, was it –' she thrust a book back into its place, punctuating the end of her explanation – already, she thought, it had gone straggling on too long as if she were trying to undermine herself. 'You can accuse me, if you want, of being insufficiently a romantic to get carried away – but then my materialism is just part of my character and I carry it around whatever I do. It wasn't just doing the wrong thing I was afraid of.'

Eleanor twirled her cigarette neatly in her fingers, round and round in the fingertips of one hand. Making something out of pain, she thought, Bea's rejection, twenty-five years old and still apparently a great shock, blossoming into this little manual dexterity.

'And if,' she said after a while, 'you were living with me now, and not with Tim, would that be all the same, no difference?'

Bea paused in her trailing progress around the edges of the room, suddenly, as if she had come up against a wall. She stood over Eleanor's chair, angry: 'No, it would not be the same – but how was I to see that, all that, then?'

Eleanor looked up: 'You weren't, of course, and what about all those years in between? You wouldn't have brought up any daughters with me. So it's as well.' She tapped ash precisely into the ashtray, 'You can still contribute to the cause of the emancipation of women, you know, as Tim's wife.' Eleanor felt cold, tired; layers and layers of cold wrapping her tired voice. She felt it wilting inside her, too tired to voice any more any of the misery. It was as well, it was all as well, she thought, why give herself the useless pain of talking about it any more? But she saw that Bea had collapsed onto the carpet by her chair, was laughing.

Bea leaned her arm across Eleanor's knees, ' "The emancipation of women",' she echoed, ' "as Tim's wife"! I'd rather stay with you.'

Eleanor looked down at her. I am so easily, so easily brought round, she thought. How dangerous it must be to have allowed myself so far, where a sentence brings me; but she felt only calm as she watched Bea. The calm of a drugged patient before the final needle, she thought. A lulled calm. 'But it's not as easy as that, is it,' she said.

* * * * * * * * * * * * * *. *

Eleanor watched her down the street to the corner, a tall blue-grey figure receding with measured steps, as if the final shot of some predictable film. Only going for a walk, Eleanor reminded herself. But the sense of irrevocable departure did not lift — she hung in the shop doorway: there were people who went down to the tobacconist's and never returned, took the dog for a stroll and melted into another identity, people who wanted to escape. But Bea could go home any time, had only to escape from saying goodbye.

Eleanor turned back into the shop and closed the door against the wind in the street: I am thinking of her as a lover, she realised, a lover again. Whose every departure might be the last, who is untrustworthy because she is carrying too much of my trust with her. She sat down slowly on a crate, feeling for the cigarettes in her overall pocket: here I am, in a moment. She lit a cigarette, watched the smoke curl up from the tip. Here I am, then. So much for the tyranny that I was to put aside, the clarity that had begun to seem insufficient to live by.

So lightly put aside — I had better kept it, it was what I had, what I had made, my ballast. Without it — Eleanor reached a hand up to her hair, her eyes running vaguely over the apples in the window — it's going to rain, she thought, noticing their dimmed colour. Yes, without my detachment; she got up to turn the light on — it was going to be a storm, perhaps. For it will end badly, must if I have made her that to me again. When she goes — how could I have done it when I know she's going? Eleanor smiled, and reached carefully out to a piece of cotton dangling from her cuff; that was it, of course, that she had decided to do just that, going or not. Had decided, in some submerged moment.

She stood up; no one out on the street. Upstairs she put the kettle on to boil, set a mug on the tray. A decision waiting for an opportunity. Made, only waiting for Bea to come. Eleanor looked around, at objects that for this moment were revealed as malleable, obliging: all within reach. The lid fits, the tray is carried lightly down the stairs, feet are sure. Activated by Bea's arrival, the last touch in the programme. I do not change so much, she thought, am in control even of my departure from control. To the last minute, the entrance, her unexpected entrance.

The tea poured, frothed, the tang of it filling the room. And if she had not come then, when I was almost ready for her? Eleanor smiled again — whatever was necessary. The pleasurable taste of tea, the ease and lightness; Eleanor looked round now, fixing the vividness of things in her mind. All this, these incidentals, these apposite details — they are all very well, she thought. Charming, even, the touch that my life lacks. But I live with my consequences. What of this fragile life, distorted by Bea, by the room I have made for her? It must have seemed that any changes would be sweeping, Eleanor thought, that must have been how I saw it. That I would be somehow swept up in a whirlwind of sensation. At the end emerge, left on some new ground by the storm, subtly altered. Eleanor considered her knobbled hands, cupped about the mug: the brown stain running along the index finger; the old ridge where a carving knife had slipped. Here I am, having taken that plunge — and still myself. What was it for, though, if not to give that old self that to get its teeth into? Not because I wanted to abandon myself, the opposite, that I wanted to give myself my due.

She walked to the window. The rain had begun to fall, not hard enough yet to drive people off the streets. They walked past the shop, glancing hurriedly at the window, but none came in. It was as if they saw in the piled fruit the dusty remnants of summer, a summer discredited now by the sharp air that hit their faces. The eager queues of the morning, sniffing at the apple crop in the sunshine, were of another season. Eleanor turned away again — it had been in part a test, perhaps. A test of her choices, and her capacities. Well, she thought, there's no doubt I can still do it. Still frighteningly capable of the same. But how much of this, that she had let herself into, that had taken her over, these feelings for Bea — how much were they memory, ordinary nostalgia? It is unimportant. There is only, here I am, with this feeling, as if knocked sideways. Leaning over drunkenly towards her, no pillars under this part of the structure.

And her leaving — what would that do? Falling apart, that was what you were afraid of. Never mind that the attachment might be made up of odd scraps of old feeling, old illusions, new veneers, whatever. Only the falling apart would matter then. And I stand here hand again on the teapot, taking pleasure in the way the liquid froths in the mug. As if there were permanence. Eleanor glanced to the window: the rain was falling steadily. Shouldn't the walk be over, she wondered, could Bea be staying out there for some reason, that she had to stay out still? In the rain — Eleanor laughed. For all this they were themselves still, and not now likely to stay out in the rain. By the same token, then, would she get by? I am a historian of myself, she thought, my own permanence. I leap in, but the perspective does not go — perhaps it is blurred for a moment. But I do not let go of my past. All that has been true for me in the past.

She took her mug to the door, watching the corners for Bea's return. But the world is nonetheless changed by it, she thought, there is little enough of what I shall always have that remains. So much that I shall have to lose. But as she stood at the door listening to the rain fall the thought of future losses had no substance.

Bea stopped by a gate. Almost at once splashes of rain began to fall on the grey wood. She looked up at a dark sky: it must have been gathering for hours as the miles went by. She felt the rain falling into her hair, heard it hitting hard dry leaves in the hedges. She looked back the way she had come — surely it was a long way. There were no trees, no overhanging hedgerows. She could only start back. The road began to darken with the rain as she walked. An old image of desolation, she thought, caught out in the rain with no shelter. Driven back. To those women. On her way she had only walked, not caring to think. And so she had turned down roads one after another, watching her feet move out in front of her, watching for the next turning. Now that she was turned back to them, she thought of them again. Sitting in the shop over their tea like calm spiders, weaving to catch her up into their lives. Dee's quiet look, so certain of her, only waiting. And Eleanor perched up on her stool, saying nothing.

She turned a corner, following a signpost. At the corner a wide gate hung open, a muddy track led up to a barn, half full of straw. Bea swung off the road towards it, out of the thickening rain. She climbed carefully onto the stack, three bales high, and crawled towards the middle. Her hands and knees sunk into sudden gaps that opened as she moved. In the centre, a small heap of bales were piled up; Bea reached them and sat, gasping, her back against the stack. Cigarettes still safe in her pocket. She sat on, listening to the loud thunder of rain on the corrugated roof. It's Friday, she thought, I ought to be at home, thinking of what we're to do over the week-end. Picking the beans. There will be so much, so much I have to do. She lit a cigarette. This cosy little refuge, the storm outside. A child's game, playing house. The fruit shop, its wooden floor, those boxes of shiny fruit, the bananas hanging in the window — that's how I see it,

Bea thought, a fairy tale illustration. There's safety in its being a fairy tale, I can see that. So I shan't have to stay where I don't belong. Those others seem to tell me that I can stay, that I do belong. And there you are — if I did, it would have to be home. Not a tale. Set about with their expectations, those women. Alien women, surely. Bea knocked ash slowly into the palm of her hand. Could she just take their code, like a new shell? Ease off the old, back carefully into the new, simply decide to accustom herself to its differences, its strangenesses? So much to learn, she thought wearily. And if I don't fit into what's left me at home, it's not that I do here. I am someone else, aren't I, after all these years? Not one of them. Not with my history.

Bea turned up the collar of her jacket and huddled back against a bale. She felt cold and hopeless, turning her back finally on what had once seemed bright and welcoming. But why try to swop one enclosure for another, when both seem as if they'll stop the flow of blood to some part of you? I don't fit here, she repeated to herself. I should have liked to, perhaps, but I don't. She lifted her head towards the roof: the drumming had died away a little, and as she sat listening the sound became that of single drops banging themselves out above her, the last of the rain.

Bea eased herself stiffly towards the side of the barn. Too old for such discomfort, and a long way back to the village. And when I get there, she thought, picking her way through the mud to the lane — what is it I'll say? How answer her, the questions she won't ask? Staring as if she saw through me. She's been hiding herself less. How she still wants — to pay attention to me. I can't go, Bea thought, hurrying along a road, her hands in her pockets, I can't leave. She listens to me. Why don't you hide yourself — I thought you would, I could see you could if you wanted, Nellie? All that coming clean to me that I asked you for — you knew I was leaving, I know you knew. And yet you've laid yourself open as if that might make a difference. But you knew that as well, didn't you — that it wouldn't. Can't have done it for that. Do you care, that it makes it harder for me, because you let me see that you would have me stay? No, Bea thought — she does not care. I am strangely irrelevant in a way. I do what I do, come and go, and she sees it and takes it and nothing stops her. Bea grimaced to herself: a cog in the wheels of Eleanor's knowledge. Eleanor in control of herself, prepared for the future. Sitting wordless on her stool, letting Dee indulge her certainty. That was this morning.

'When the shop shuts, then.' Eleanor straightened herself and began to sweep again. The floor would need washing, though, with all the rain. Ash mixed in, now. A grey paste in a minute if she didn't sweep. All this was to be expected — he'd be wanting her at the week-end. 'You'd better find out what the times are, tell him you're coming, hadn't you? 'Phone box is in the square.' She glanced over at Bea, standing motionless at the window, head turned to the road, 'You should get changed first, though, get out of those wet clothes. Time for a bath, water's hot — why not have one?' How many more things can I think to say at this level, she wondered. I could probably keep it up until she leaves, could be quite fun, a challenge. Talk for hours without saying anything. She'd be glad to go, then — and why should I say anything that matters? I can say it to myself later and save us both trouble.

Bea lifted her head: 'I have to go, Eleanor,' she said, 'I'm no part of this, you know. I've been doing something so different for so long —' she turned away again, 'it's irrevocable.'

Eleanor checked her broom for a moment, 'I know you have to go. I'm tired of talking about it, while you stand there dripping muddy water onto the floor and trying to get pneumonia.'

Bea shrugged: 'I'll go and 'phone then.'

She leant against the red bars and listened as Tim's switchboard sorted through their calls.

'What've you got on there?' thin voices kept asking, 'That one's not still holding, is it?'

Tim had said the operators were inefficient, she remembered, due for reorganisation.

'I like your switchboard girls,' she said when he came through, 'will you tell them?'

Tim laughed, 'What would I say? "My wife likes you"?'

'Something like that.'

'But Bea, what would it mean?'

He was right, of course — it could not be said. 'I'm coming back this evening,' she went on, 'be at the station about nine, can you pick me up? Or there are taxis —'

'I'll fetch you — have you had a good time? Meet anyone?'

Bea shook her head at the receiver: 'I'll tell you all about it when I see you, dear, I'm in a 'phone box now.'

There was a lot that could not be said, it seemed. When she hung up, it was with a sense of things having slightly altered. Of course she had never divulged everything to Tim, what would he have done with it all? Found it irrelevant or boring, or perhaps incomprehensible. It wasn't a new absence. She had always acknowledged the need for reticence. She stood outside the box, looking round the square. War memorial, railings, petrol station. A wind that had plastered sheets of half-scrumpled newspaper up against the railings. She walked over towards the memorial. The thing was, she realised, that the area of reticence seemed suddenly to have grown. As if Eleanor and her friends and all they stood for had thrust themselves into her life even as she was leaving them. There they were, standing about in her mind, a part of her past. Pointing at switchboard operators. Whispering, 'Who did you meet?' Should she tell Tim, then? Would he want to know? Should she tell him anyway?

She walked round the concrete plinth, names set out without rank. Equality in death; or more likely that they were all of them privates. He still wouldn't want to hear, she knew. It had only been a visit, a three-day visit. She'd said to him once, she'd been sorry when the war ended, almost, had liked the excitement and the important darkness. Yes, he'd said, I was fifteen and in the OTC. Not wanting to know about that, either. She lingered, her shoulders hunched, watching a couple of cars pulling in for petrol. A decent privacy: he required it. Don't I, she wondered, expect it too − not to be too delved into? Eleanor a few yards down the road, sweeping as if she could put me with the other rubbish into a pile and scoop it into the dustbin. Larding herself now with layer after layer, her privacy. No, she thought, I don't really want to be so secretive, to embrace the necessity for it like this. A car drove off suddenly, its petrol cap falling with a clatter to the forecourt. A woman came out of the building and bent slowly to pick it up, letting the car draw out into the street unimpeded. Yes, Bea thought, let them all get on with it.

She walked through the shop; Eleanor was dropping oranges into someone's bag. I never asked her how much she makes, she thought, climbing the stairs. The cat squawked on the landing, and eyed her, turning towards the kitchen. Bea walked on into her room. She undressed, leaving her clothes piled in the centre of her bed. The suit she had been wearing hung in the cupboard. She put it on again. The skirt she had bought to wear the night before lay on a chair: I must take them away with me, she thought, but I shall need a bag to hold them all.

She went down; Eleanor stood in the doorway, her hands by her sides, her back to the shop. At the sight of her Bea stopped, caught again by something — that thinness, the shapeless flattened cloth at her knees. She had taken off her overall, was closing up. She is not so easy to leave. Fragments come out at me. Her loosened skin. Those bony hands. Thought even the memory had gone, the precise memory of sensation. A trick perhaps, an imaginative reconstruction, nothing of the present in it. Bea lowered herself onto the stool by the till. It seems real enough.

'Do you have a plastic bag?' she said.

Eleanor waved towards a corner without turning round, 'Over there, piles of them.'

Bea wanted her to turn around. 'I like you ever so much more without your overall,' she said at last.

Eleanor laughed: 'You're merciless,' she said, over her shoulder.

I should go back upstairs, Bea thought, does she know that I wanted to see her face? It must be getting late, almost time to leave. In the silence they could hear the cat begin to call at the head of the stairs. She would be off now, any minute, putting things into saucers.

'Nellie —'

'What is it?'

She had turned round. I have a train to catch, Bea thought, what am I doing poking myself like this, seeing if I twitch? The train leaves in an hour. She shook her head, 'Nothing.'

The landscape unrolled; all partings at railway stations are the same, she thought. Provided with a special significance out of some store we all carry: leaving for the front, for the city, his last journey. Evacuees with labels. It is always better to be the one on the train, not the woman left on the platform with the limp handkerchief. Leaving is hopeful: we hide a smile of anticipation as the doors slam. So I am somehow convinced that I am returning to some new venture. That there will be something to say at the other end. She took one of the unopened cigarettes from the top of the carrier bag; we didn't smoke enough, she thought, it would have been worth doing not to have to take these away with me like unwanted presents. The scene is littered with tired old associations, symbolic little rejections.

She turned to the window. It was as if she were moving backwards through country that the other day had been opening up before her. She put an unlit cigarette down on the seat beside her and leant back, closing her eyes wearily. She was too tired now to think of what there might be to do next, of how to take up again the things she had dropped gladly to come here, thinking it might be some answer.

* * * * * * * * * * * * * * * *

Eleanor drove further, on past the village towards a line of hills that she had once seen on the map. There was a path that ran along the ridge — there would be views up there, and a wind.

She left the car in a gravelled clearing. There was no one else there to read the boards set out with different colours. I should have been before, she thought, choosing in the end the shortest route — or perhaps I will come again. She grinned, clambering over the first stile — a transparent attempt to suggest that there could be continuity in my life. Treating myself carefully, so carefully, now. You don't want to go home just yet? Then you shan't. A nice walk, just one of lots of things you could do, Eleanor, to halt this brooding you're so inclined to. And the walk did seem as if it might be pleasant, after all.

The path led through a beech wood, and as she walked Eleanor became aware of the silence. She stopped, and heard only the faint sound of the wind above and the rattle of beechnuts falling from a tree nearby. She had been right to come; the trees were more than a consolation, they were solid creatures from some quite other state of mind. It was as if in the air between them her thoughts had to run on a different, a wider, smoother track, could almost only think how very beautiful and silent they were, these trees. And so she walked on lightly, suspended between the soothing trunks on either side.

But the wood began to thin as the path climbed towards the hilltop; Eleanor came out soon onto a steep grassy slope, and the brow of the hill ahead of her. She left the exhilaration of the beeches behind her, trudging through the grass. Breaking out, she thought, there hadn't been so much of that, after all. She arrived too quickly. Before I've half thought where it might or might not be leading me. She arrives — like a gift, maybe, but one I wasn't quite ready for. But there could be no waiting. Like unripe fruit when there's a frost coming. Pick it and hope that somehow there'll be a use. It might ripen, in time. Plenty of time, when she's gone. And now she's gone, of course.

She had come out on the top of the hill, and into the wind. She stood, watching the grass around her bend and whip up as gusts came and died away. The path led on towards the other side of the hill, already almost dark. Eleanor followed, leaving the view unseen. Somehow I was expecting more, she thought, expecting it to add up to more than those three days. For it all has to end now; if it wasn't Bea that began it, it's she who has the ending of it. I have spent myself on her, directed myself at her and I can't divert any more. If she hadn't come, it might have been different. I should have had longer to think, perhaps I would have decided on − but there didn't seem so much else. It was only that she felt cheated that it had happened so fast. You might have thought there would have been no hurry, if anything were to change after all this time, she thought, hurrying down the hill.

This rush, as if I didn't have the rest of my life ahead of me still. She stopped to eat a few blackberries hanging over the next stile, still bright from the rain. Do you have to be going backwards, Nellie, always trying to relive something in order to get it right? She sat down on the damp stile and lit a cigarette; surely I meant to do better than that, was only going over the old stuff before I went on? It had all become too tied up with people, she thought. Too much Ann and Dee as well as Bea. They had only been a starting point, after all, something to consider. No one was indispensable. And she had fallen into thinking that they were, of hinging things onto them in the flesh as if it all stood or fell by their presence. But of course she did not need them, could use them or do without them. Or that was how it had always been, wasn't it, a way of standing alone and seeing what was to be done without needing more than she could get?

But that other way. That way of living that she had been thinking of as if it might be worth trying for − that called for distinctions between people. Selecting those who were worth more than the observations you might make about them. And it meant engaging yourself with them, being prepared to bear the dependence on them. It was a risk.

Eleanor stretched out to flick ash on the ground: perhaps it was as well that Bea had appeared so suddenly. She might so easily never have brought herself to the point, given time to go on weighing the dangers. Now, again, it was too dangerous, with Beatrice gone. Those other two were a luxury, Eleanor saw, things for a rich and prosperous season. It was not the time for expansion any more, or for experiments.

I am a desert animal, she thought, adapted for life in barren places. I should have learned to be suspicious of fleshy blooms by now, and to expect only rocks, with which I can get on well enough. A very specialised species. She stood up and walked on; the paths were beginning to converge. She could see the blue of the van through the hedge. As a life-form, she thought, I am a stop-gap. Something very hardy whose only brilliance is in survival. The kind that in any utopia fades out before anything, its skills useless and outdated and even a little disgusting. Something too desperate and a little crude about us.

She awoke to a diffused light. It is much worse than that, she thought. Not simply a matter of taking things up where I left off. I have let myself grow into these extensions. I have begun to think of them as part of what I can expect of a day. That was the worse, the dailiness, the simple getting up, going down: that was all now to be part of the withdrawal. Not safe to let Ann and Dee in now. It was a matter of survival, nothing lovely or sensible about it. She sat up abruptly to look at her watch and heard the cat jump down from the table outside the door.

'Yes, I'm awake, but it's early,' she said, as the cat appeared beside the bed. Why a cat, she wondered, watching her sit down and half-close her eyes, what is the point to me of this cat? She scares the birds I should like to have watched in the garden. I should be rid of her too.

Eleanor settled back onto her pillows; but this is not something I care about this morning. I probably have her for her habits, her regularity — something to mark the passage of time with. But I shall need better than that as a distraction. I had better ask, why myself. She got out of bed and began to feel her way down the stairs to the kitchen. It seemed to be a time for keeping going, a deadened cycle. Feed the cat, pour another kettle of water into the tea-pot. She put the water on and turned upstairs again. An old robot, she thought, snapping plastic teeth into place between the real ones, a little less than human this morning. But still here; she bared the completed teeth at the mirror — and not thinking of leaving. Was it pointless, her inevitable hanging on? Could never get past the same memory, her hands gripping the bedstead, don't let them put the curtains round me Nellie. Odd that it was the only death she had seen. Perhaps they were often like that, she thought, and really no reason not to be able to go sooner if it seemed best. It had not reached that yet, that was all.

She went downstairs again to make the tea, carried the pot into the front room. The morning was disintegrating into a few fragments, a series of small efforts to dull the edge of the coming day. So that was what was needed, she thought climbing up to dress, all that was possible. A dreary progress from possible to possible. It was not even possible to wear anything different — she got into the same clothes.

It would have been better if Dee weren't coming this morning. If she didn't have to be dealt with just yet, all her talk and her expectant look. Eleanor sighed, but she should have learned already, rather than my having to go about dealing blows. Bea had left so much mess behind — going lightly back cocooned as she had arrived by her own necessities. How little Bea's detachment had mattered, though, how unreal that other existence of hers had seemed. Eleanor walked wearily down the stairs, holding the banister. It was going to be a long day. She noticed that the sun had come out, and was dimly lighting the staircase.

* * * * * * * * * * * * * * *

'Do you have anything planned for today?' Tim lifted the lid of the coffee pot and poured the last of the coffee into his cup. Even on this Saturday morning, the week-end before him, his movements were precise and appropriate. He lifted his head enquiringly at his wife.

'I was going to see what needed doing in the garden,' Bea said. She vaguely felt him to be carefully approaching some distant goal. 'Can you think of something more exciting?'

Tim shook his head very slightly and raised his cup. 'Quite a bit needs doing, I should think,' he said after a while, the coffee held gently in front of him, 'all those fruit trees still have to be picked.'

Bea's finger drew patterns in the crumbs on her plate. 'I shall pick what I need and then the people around here who haven't any can come and pick their own.'

Tim set the cup down again, 'No one can be bothered to pick their own any more, Bea, you know it never works in the end.'

'So they stay on the tree.' Bea heaped the crumbs carefully into a pile.

'It seems a waste, though, doesn't it,' Tim said reasonably.

Bea looked at the packet of cigarettes beside her. I can hold off those for a while, she thought.

'We don't need so much,' Time was saying, 'now that the children have left –'

'They've been gone for years,' Bea objected, hearing him moving on, reaching inexorably on.

'But now that you want to go back to work, Bea, there won't be time for all that gardening and this big house too.' Tim looked down from the ceiling and directly at Bea across the table, 'You can see that I'm right – we need something small, with all the modern devices. And just a bit of lawn or something.'

'But your vegetables.'

'Make a clean break. I'll move on to something else.'

Bea reached for the cigarettes, took one out, lit it, leant back to stare upwards: 'I expect you might be. Right,' she said. It did seem sensible; perhaps it was only the way he had described the house, as if he saw it as something box-like, deliberately box-like. And she had always liked small gardens. She noticed Tim's hand playing with his cup, turning it round and round on its saucer, a demonstration of control.

'It's really long past breakfast,' she said, flicking ash next to the heap of crumbs.

'We can't sit over any meal without your lighting up.'

'I was trying to keep off them — but then you go and tell me we're moving house.'

'I don't know why you're so hostile to the idea.' Tim let his hand fall hopelessly away from the cup.

Bea shrugged: 'Perhaps I only need to think about it.'

She walked under the plum tree, raising a hand to the over-loaded branches. Of course there were too many, even in a bad year were too many. She pulled off a plum and let it fall to the ground. Time to pass all this on to people with schemes for jam making, to people who still ate jam. This predictable reluctance to shut down your activities, admit that something has become irrelevant with age. Tim is right, and I shall find myself a job, concentrate on something else. She sat down on a tree stump. It was difficult to imagine that new place: vague and empty in her mind, as empty as her plans. They would both be leaving it, early in the morning, this new house; often coming back to it only in the dark, wanting to lie in front of the television with the lights off everywhere. That kind of house, the centre of no one's day.

Bea sighed; that would be a relief in a way, not to have to carry this out-sized construction, this family home where every surface, each old jam jar, wore an accretion of significance and memory, someone else's past. She thought of the two of them, in the new place, filled with what they had brought back from the city, sleeping over before going back, thoughts turned towards it. Bea looked at that picture curiously: she couldn't quite see herself in it — surely she wouldn't launch herself so far in? Even if an opportunity offered? But it was either that, she thought, or a sort of uneasy half-life, an attempt to make a functional house something beyond itself. She looked round at the sagging trees; I must try to see, she thought, what will come in its place when I draw away from here. It will have to be different, come differently than all this that I slid into, an imperceptible series that someone else had set ready for me.

The image of herself and Tim sitting over some table, hunched with mercantile thoughts, returned, an unexplained vision. Something that she feared. She felt the shiny table, the silence between them. They seemed to be turning away, to the side, towards something half-seen beyond them. Their attention was not on each other, but on this other creature. Not human, something metallic about it; but they seemed to speak to it, angrily. Something about the quality of the service, Bea understood, everything should be ready. Their time was being wasted. And all the time, as the words flared, she could see in their minds schemes being turned over, options set out and rejected; the two at each side of the table were building patterns as complex as circuitry in their heads. Bea shook herself — an absurd transformation. What was she afraid of, she wondered, in this change, that her imagination turned it into a nightmare of whirling machinery? She looked up and started, finding Tim on the path in front of her, his look considering.

'You haven't decided against getting a job, have you?'

'I haven't got one yet,' Bea said, 'I don't know how easy it's going to be —'

'They're crying out for good secretaries!' Tim looked her over again; would he, he wondered, employ her? There was that about her, a wilfulness, might make them cautious. Or perhaps she knew better than to let that show, away from here.

'I'm sure you could sell yourself,' he said. Bea nodded. Tim went on, feeling her resistance but seeing so clearly the sense of it all that he must set out — what they could have. If only they thought it out, thought what they wanted, planned. 'With a small modern house,' he explained, 'we'd be much freer, don't you see? To come and go, to devote our time to things outside — not tied down by always having to be there for one thing or another —'

Bea watched him, wondering vaguely what things outside he wanted to devote so much time to. Surely this house didn't impinge on him so much, she thought. It's I who spend my time here, and now he wants me to stop, for some reason. His vegetables. My house, our garden. The connections between us are only there, she realised. And now we are to move away from them. She did not know quite what to make of that: it had been something that had not entered into her calculations.

* * * * * * * * * * * * * * *

Dee found Eleanor washing the floor, the boards wet to the shop doorway and Eleanor way off at the other side of the room. She hung in the doorway: 'Hello, shouldn't I be doing that?'

Eleanor went on with the mopping, 'I was up early,' she said, glad of the floor between them. 'Bea left last night, asked me to say goodbye to you.' She glanced at Dee across the room: 'As expected. Let's not talk about it, shall we?'

Dee stood still for a little: 'I'll just sit here and have a cigarette, then, until the floor's dry.' She sat on the step and stuck her feet out onto the pavement. Expected? She had not known what to expect. And knowing it might be going to happen made no difference. That Eleanor with Bea gone again would be like this, putting her at such a distance — perhaps that was to have been expected. Dee pulled the cigarettes out of her pocket, wanting to be able to crush the packet between her hands, throw stones in the road. This whole episode had been so much out of her control, from the start: she had only stood by, letting herself be affected by events. Eleanor had always gone on, doing as she wanted, not caring what might happen to her, how she might feel. And now she simply chose to close down, refuse to discuss. Dee pushed open the matchbox upside down and watched as the matches rolled about on the pavement. She picked one up to light her cigarette.

Like a child, she thought, and bent down to gather the matches out of the dust, expecting confidence. She turned to lean her back against the door lintel and watched the thrust of the mop across the room. It was too like a Saturday morning at home, playing on the kitchen floor while the hoover banged into the furniture in the next room; too like that, she felt, for this being shut out to be anything but temporary. She would switch it off in a moment and sigh, and through the open door Dee would see her wipe her forehead with the back of her hand. She would come through and fling open the new refrigerator for orange squash and pour out two glasses. Then the kettle, for tea because the dust made you thirsty, and after that the shopping trolley from under the stairs and out into the street with their coats. Dee looked out into the street: it was beginning, delivery vans all down the road, bread coming out in packages; nothing like shopping on a Saturday morning with the queues everywhere and the baskets and trolleys banging each other in the street and knocking over the bicycles in the gutter, and the doughnut in Lyons afterwards.

'It's more or less dry now,' Eleanor called.

Dee turned reluctantly, 'Shall I make a cup of tea?' she asked, thinking somehow that if she could only reproduce the conditions, Eleanor too would sit down and put the hoovering behind her, the worst of the day over.

'I've only just had some,' Eleanor said, her hands turning over the bundles in the till, 'don't make me any.'

'Do you ever have a holiday?' Dee asked, thinking how she would like to be deep in a huge city supermarket now, racks and racks of things to choose from and a houseful of people to shop for, with money enough to rifle the sweets while she stood in the queue: 'Do you ever close up and go shopping or anything?'

Eleanor closed the till quietly and looked curiously at Dee, standing looking out into the street. I suppose she thinks I should get away from it all. Forget my troubles, as if to think about them is morbid instead of necessary. As if forgetting's something I want to do. 'I don't like shopping,' she said.

'Oh, I do, buying things. I miss that about my old job, the ritual evening shop once a week.'

Eleanor smiled faintly. Dee making conversation.

She watched her leave with relief when it was time at last, and shut the door behind her, turning the card in the window. She ate bread and cheese, dropping crumbs onto the carpet of the front room. The violin, when she took it out of its case, was out of tune. Probably sharp, she decided, when it was ready and she had found some music, an old part score that would sound a little thin and fitful played on its own. But the sounds were strange and pleasing, nonetheless. Nothing of getting away in this, she thought, no pointless holiday. An addition, it says what I know, what I must remember.

Dee walked slowly, picking dusty blackberries as she went. She found Ann crouched over the gate with a paint brush.

'What are you painting it for?'

Ann shrugged: 'So it doesn't rot during the winter, I suppose. And the sun was shining.'

'Don't tell me I'm stuck out here until the paint dries, for god's sake.'

'Of course not – there you are.' Ann stood up and poked the gate open with her brush, 'What's the matter?'

'Beatrice has left and Eleanor has lapsed into silence.' Dee walked away down the path.

Ann turned back to the gate: so the bright lady from sunny suburbia was gone, then. Stayed just long enough to cause a sufficient disturbance. Going back with such news, what an insight into how the other half lives. You never know, do you, when you drop in on these old friends, quite what you'll find – turned to all kinds of things, some of them. Meditations, curious little sects. All sorts of consolations, and tell you it's a way of life, the true path even. And Eleanor – some odd friends, very odd. What you do behind your bedroom door of course, but there's no need – Ann dabbed undercoat carefully into the corners.

An adventurous Beatrice, holidaying from the real world like a city dweller ogling arcane practices. Not the sort of thing you could give a talk on, perhaps, back home. Good for the more serious dinners, though, see them attack their salmon mousse with renewed vigour, is that so? well you never know in this world, do you? In the middle of the night, something to comfort herself with – there but for. I might have been. Did they call it gay, now, little jokes, think it the thing to say about respectable men. Forster and ballet dancers. Think it will do for women too, if they could think of any. Do you remember Nancy Spain, my dear?

Ann eyed the gate post doubtfully. It could really do with more drastic treatment, down to the wood. She ran her hand up it, a decent piece of wood underneath, something someone had worked gently, once. She dipped her brush in the pot, another item of domestic architecture degenerating. They were always the same, these women, ready to pretend they saw you, oh they quite saw your point of view and no, nothing would change, would it, unless women tore themselves free. And you could see their eyebrows lift at that, as if they saw themselves clasped in someone's arms, struggling for a moment – and then saw that they could not any more, struggle – it was where they belonged. And of course they do belong, they do – Ann swept the brush up and down the length of the post – things work very well with them squashed into those cosy places.

She shuffled round to the far side of the post; not going to make it a regular thing, are you, Beatrice? Come back once in a while to dazzle us with the prize of you, something to play for? Never mind how long the odds are, isn't she worth it, what has she come for, if it isn't to cross over? A good game, good for a long time yet, because we never can quite afford to close the door on her. Any woman can change her mind, her life, isn't that what we think? She sat back on her heels and eyed the post. It was going to soak straight through, more than likely. No more than a patching job, even with the gloss on. She stood up and propped the gate open again with a stone. Anyone coming might still touch it, she thought, looking down – but there was no one expected.

She put the paint down on the kitchen table and looked over Dee's shoulder, 'You're doing the crossword again.'

'Good for the nerves.'

'Were you expecting her to stay then? Doesn't it seem a bit unlikely that she would? Just like that?' Ann sat down and drew the bread board towards her. She leant back, sawing at the air with the knife, full of the inevitability of the departure, every woman's departure to safety: 'That doesn't happen any more, women making these political gestures. It's yesterday's extremism. Everybody's too worried about their futures or their pensions or being without protection from rapists –'

Dee threw the paper aside, 'No doubt. That's not the point at all. God knows what the general picture is anyway – just because they aren't leaving their husbands for you any longer.' Dee considered Ann across the table – as far as that went they still would if she asked, she thought. Always a few who saw the romance of it, all the better if it wasn't quite what everyone was doing. 'The thing is not that Bea is yet another example of just what you'd expect – the point is her out of her damn context, that particular Bea. Eleanor thought she'd stay, Ann, that's the thing.'

Ann put down the knife, and looked at it: 'She can't really have thought she would?'

'She wouldn't talk about it. She didn't say that, she said it was expected.'

Ann rolled a piece of bread along the table top. Eleanor at the table, over dinner that night. She had been watching Beatrice, watching her warily, surely. A prodigal returned who might so easily have become a double agent. There was that sense of their being aware of the chasm between them every minute of the time. Ann shook her head: 'I can't believe she really thought that, she was much too distant.'

Dee dragged over the bread and began to cut herself a slice, 'Well, this morning she was much worse — something must have made her retreat like that.'

'Presumably even if she knew the woman was bound to go back home she would still have been upset by it.'

Dee took the slice of bread out of her mouth and chewed impatiently, 'I know that, for god's sake.' She stared down at the table. Ann's scepticism had made her lose hold of the significance of this morning's long, deliberate silences. There had been more there than her intrusion on Eleanor's private misery. Something more. 'I just think,' she said slowly, 'that Bea's going has made a difference to how Eleanor feels about us. That she might be about to reject us.'

'It's a bit early to tell, isn't it?' Ann tilted her chair back and balanced herself against the table with her foot, 'You know,' she said, 'it would have been nice, to have her here as well. I begin to feel as if I'm more peculiar than I really am, if I knew what that was any more. They're so very normal up here, so very family, so deep in the right women's magazines. All the girls go through just the right phases. And the only way that anything goes against just what is expected of everybody, it's by having too many children, or living in horrible poverty. Just think, with Beatrice here, how respectable I'd feel. We could have spent a lot of time trying to pretend our differences were unimportant and that we weren't alone any more.'

'We haven't done very much about that — being alone, have we?' Dee stood up: 'It all seems very predictable now, doesn't it. I think I'll go and do some weeding or something out there.'

The bunch of weeds scratched the palm of her hand. Dee shuffled her heels along the path. This might have been one of the things she'd come for; she couldn't remember. Plenty of things they'd come from; what had they seen here, though? As if it was real life that went on here. Because it was not theirs, they'd thought it was real. You had to start with the real, the solid lives, ordinary. Dee grimaced: that was Ann's way of seeing, that had rather taken over. My life is solid and ordinary enough, she thought, no problem blending me in with the mass. But Ann — dangerously outside, she thought herself, always hovering on the edge of being discounted altogether. The country for her was to be a kind of raw material. And she would arrive among them, these untouched women. Going about into their meeting places and getting in on their cups of coffee. Ann taking them, real and solid, and moulding them a little, until they would fit her, until she would fit amongst them. Still real, so that Ann shouldn't feel she wasn't earthed any more, but a little changed, coloured by Ann's presence and her ideas. That had not happened.

Dee paused, resting her hands on her knees; it was as final as that, she realised, uncurling her fingers to look at the squashed bundle of yellow and green that expanded a little in the palm of her hand, it had not happened. There had never been the opening that, surely, should have come. There had been nothing, no one, they could join. Dee inched forward again. It was bound to take time, longer than they'd thought. In the shop, she hung on, collecting the women's bright polite smiles. How polite they were, with their little easy anecdotes and their neat, noticing compliments. You have had a good wash here this morning. Wish I could get mine like that. And that was all. A fence they had decked out with inoffensive notices, a fence they didn't even have to think about. Dee got to her feet and carried the weeds over to the charred patch in the corner that must once have been a bonfire. She looked down at it; they hadn't used it, hadn't been able to find anything to burn. A handful of weeds, in a summer. What were they keeping that should have gone up in flames, she wondered.

Ann let the chalk drop from between her fingers. Autumn. When all there was in your mind was a heap of leaves and the cold coming into your bones. She put the pad aside on the bed and went to the window. And this landscape is going to do autumn badly, she thought, slow and grey. And relentless, as if it knew how you hated it and wanted to grind you into the mud of it. Every autumn, the same compensations. They begin to pall — toasting crumpets over the electric fire again as if I were seventeen, and the thrill of the bars shorting any moment. They pall, and I go on with them because autumn has nothing else and I have to get through it one way or another. And it's coming, though you can't quite see it yet and it pretends to be late summer. You can't miss it, living out here.

She turned back to the room, quiet and dusty in the horizontal afternoon sun; like other places she had holed up in, good enough for that. The fire still parked in the middle of the room. From the spring, when it had been cold up here in the daytime. So that you could sit on the floor and lean against the bed. What I've always lived in, she thought, rooms to hide away in. Camping out another season. Times when I've put pots on the window sills, my posters with the others on the stairs. But it's never a place to stay, all the same. Base camps, maybe, places only to sit out the bad weather; already thinking of the next. Always moving on, on to the top. No one lives long in base camps. They go home to the real places waiting. Isn't done to spend all your life moving from one to another as if you have your mind fixed on other things, some distant goal. One of these places is supposed to become permanent, living in it done willingly. Not holed up.

Perhaps I don't try, she thought, I need to think that I am in transit. I don't nail the posters to the wall. But here — in the garden there is the earth I have turned where the broad beans were. The gate needs a top coat of paint. I have promised to carve something for Eleanor's shop window. All these things weigh me down to this particular place. She took tobacco out of her pocket and began to roll a cigarette, the dry flakes falling on the carpet. That is why I did them, isn't it, to make that difference between here and the other places.

* * * * * * * * * * * * * * *

'Collecting for the harvest festival, Miss Hardy.'

Eleanor turned away from the box of plums and wiped her hands on her overall.

'It's not until next week, of course, but if I can have an idea of what you might like to give?'

Eleanor looked around: 'Well, what would you like? I've plenty of most things.'

The woman sighed, and brought a notebook out of her coat pocket, 'I've plenty of jam, already. That's not your line, of course.' She ran her finger down the page, mouth working a little as she reread the entries. 'Not very good so far this year, I'm afraid — not been a good harvest, you know.' She folded the book back into her pocket: 'I'd say you have a free hand, Miss Hardy.'

Eleanor put her head on one side: 'You'll be getting apples, I suppose. And plums.'

She became animated again, her hands floating briefly in the air: 'Oh, yes, apples and plums — we always have those on the bough, they go down very well with the decorators.'

Eleanor's eye caught the green ridged leaves in the window. They weren't all going to be sold by next week, and a little old already. 'Corn on the cob, then,' she said, pointing.

The woman looked at them doubtfully, taking out her notebook. 'We'll be coming to collect next Saturday afternoon.' She waved slightly as she turned to step out of the door: 'Lovely day, Miss Hardy.'

Eleanor turned back to the plums, they were going mushy, not being bought. They would have to make compost, boxes of compost. She picked up the first of the musty boxes and turned towards the back of the shop.

* * * * * * * * * * * * * * *

Ann switched on the fire and leant back against the bed. She watched as the bars began to glow, fading out the rest of the room.

'Dee,' she called, 'Dee! What're you doing?' She heard Dee get off the bed and walk to the door.

'I'm pretending to read,' Dee said, 'I thought you were working.'

'Why don't you come and talk to me. The fire's on.'

The sound now of Dee turning back into the room, the rattle as she picked up her cigarettes and matches off the table, her feet on the floorboards again, and the door opening. Ann made room by the fire, waited while Dee sat down, put her cigarettes on the carpet, fitted her back against the bed. After a moment, Ann picked up the hand that lay next to hers and held it. Dee smiled a little and looked into the fire, feeling the hot air on her eyes.

'We seem to be cocooned in our private miseries,' Ann remarked.

Dee nodded: 'I don't know what it is with you,' she said, 'you've said even less.'

Ann stretched her legs a little towards the fire, 'There's nothing special that I can name.' She tangled her fingers into Dee's: 'I don't think that whatever's bothering me would matter if it weren't for you being like this.'

Dee shrugged. She made an effort, it seemed an enormous effort. As if her thoughts were at a great remove from speech, words that even Ann could understand. It was all sunk in her mind, it must be beyond reach. She couldn't, surely, describe — all that. She only knew it, by now.

'You really want to know,' she said at last. Ann laced her fingers. After a while Dee began to speak. 'It's Eleanor. She won't speak to me, hasn't spoken to me since Bea went. Just polite, nothing else. No interest in us any more. Like a fly in the street, not worth noticing.' She paused, went on: 'And it isn't going to change, however long we wait. She's made up her mind. Must have when Beatrice first went.'

Her free hand reached out to the cigarettes. Ann took the one Dee offered her and stared deliberately at the tip. It could not be, she thought, it could not be like this. Bea had only been gone a little while, things could change. She felt the hard stone resistance to that in Dee beside her; Dee had made up her mind, it wasn't going to change. Ann inhaled and decided, that would have to be accepted.

'Why, though, why's she doing it?'

Dee shook her head: 'I thought perhaps, she felt it was our fault, her taking Beatrice in like that.'

'That's crap, Dee, it has nothing to do with us. We don't even know — that she did.'

Dee shrugged again: 'We're a kind of associated model, and have to be scrapped, you know, if things don't work out. I can't explain.'

Ann dug her heel angrily into the carpet. Blame Beatrice, shouldn't she. I'm walking backwards to, watch me retreat into my fruit shop.

'Shit,' she said.

'She has to get by.'

'Without us? I don't see that we're so damaging to her equilibrium.'

Dee fought carefully her desire to withdraw, now, to let herself be dragged back into a quiet uncommunicated despair. 'Yes,' she said, 'look at us without her. I don't think we can do without her. We've let ourselves get too involved, somehow.' She let her head fall onto Ann's shoulder, 'It's ridiculous, isn't it, but she's what this place means to me, now. And I don't know how to get back from that. As if being here was drained of meaning. As if I've spread myself out somehow and the support's suddenly gone from under me and I can't keep myself up.'

* * * * * * * * * * * * * * *

The afternoon was wet. Lights were on in the shops, and people dashed between them with umbrellas — but cheerfully, as if this were not real, were an amusing pretence at rain and wind. Ann pushed open the door: she could hear Eleanor's feet hurrying along the passage above.

'It's only Ann and Dee,' she called.

Eleanor had stopped at the head of the stairs. The banisters creaked in the silence. 'I'll bring some tea down then.' The footsteps retreated into the kitchen.

'I don't want her to have to give us tea,' Dee muttered, standing beside Ann in the empty room.

'I wish she had ashtrays.' Ann stuffed her tobacco back into her pocket. Dee paused at the entrance to the back room. The chairs in the middle; they would need them. She picked them up quickly; this was private territory again.

Eleanor set down the tray. 'We've come to say goodbye,' Ann said at once, 'we're leaving.'

Eleanor poured milk into three mugs: 'That's very sudden.'

'Not really,' Dee spoke deliberately, settling into her chair, 'we're not good at isolation.'

At self-sufficiency, thought Ann. At being you. We thought it was easy. Or natural, perhaps. Not something you have to spend your life at.

'Isolation,' Eleanor repeated, 'where will you go then?'

'Back to town.'

'There isn't anywhere else,' Ann said.

'Take your tea, Ann. You won't be alone there.'

They shook their heads; there seemed little else. They sat on over the tea. 'We're going next week,' Dee offered. Even that, she thought, why should she want to know?

'Do you want to work until you go? It's as you like.'

Dee stood up, put her mug down on the tray: 'I think I won't then, if it's all the same.'

At the door Ann turned, 'Independence,' she said, 'do you think it's teachable? We may all have to learn to live like you.'

Eleanor seemed to shrug slightly: 'You've plenty of time.'

* * * * * * * * * * * * * * *

The line hummed; there was no sound from the switch-board. Perhaps, Bea thought, they have already been reorganised. The connection clicked suddenly: 'Hello, Tim? I've made up my mind. You can put it on the market. But don't forget it's half mine.'

'And what does that mean?'

'I'm not too sure,' Bea said, 'but I think you should bear it in mind.' She let the tin voice of one of the switchboard girls cut them off.